# 'There's mo

'You speak as if
Nikolai commen

'But why?' Mallory stared at him, bewildered anew. 'What've you done?'

'It is what I have not done.' He seized the opening she had given him. 'I have not told the police about you. I have not told anyone at all that you are with me!'

**Dear Reader**

*Dobar den*! We welcome you to Bulgaria, an outstandingly beautiful country, and invite you to revel in the excitement of being somewhere just that little bit different. Relax on the sun-drenched beaches of Duni, and then travel west to the Valley of the Roses, where pink and white blossoms stretch as far as the eye can see, and enjoy all the fun of the carnival there. Rediscover romance. . .Eastern European style. *Dovizhdane*!

*The Editor*

**The author says:**

'When I knew Bulgaria, I was recently married and younger than Mallory. Looking back, I can hardly believe they were us, those two who strolled in Sofia's parks and boulevards, enjoyed its operas and concerts and open-air cafés, walked and skied on beautiful Mount Vitosa, and waited before the Cathedral at Easter for the holy flame to light the world. We still have our appreciation of the vigorous language and the complex folk-music and dancing, but where did youth go? Ah, well. We can't always be young, but this part of heaven is still there to be visited. While you are organising your journey to it, read what happened to Mallory when she went there. . .'

*Jessica Marchant*

★ TURN TO THE BACK PAGES OF THIS BOOK FOR *WELCOME TO EUROPE*. . .OUR FASCINATING FACT-FILE ★

# A PART OF HEAVEN

BY
JESSICA MARCHANT

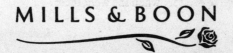

MILLS & BOON LIMITED
ETON HOUSE, 18-24 PARADISE ROAD
RICHMOND, SURREY TW9 1SR

*All the characters in this book have no existence outside the imagination of the Author, and have no relation whatsoever to anyone bearing the same name or names. They are not even distantly inspired by any individual known or unknown to the Author, and all the incidents are pure invention.*

*All Rights Reserved. The text of this publication or any part thereof may not be reproduced or transmitted in any form or by any means, electronic or mechanical, including photocopying, recording, storage in an information retrieval system, or otherwise, without the written permission of the publisher.*

*This book is sold subject to the condition that it shall not, by way of trade or otherwise, be lent, resold, hired out or otherwise circulated without the prior consent of the publisher in any form of binding or cover other than that in which it is published and without a similar condition including this condition being imposed on the subsequent purchaser.*

*First published in Great Britain 1993
by Mills & Boon Limited*

© Jessica Marchant 1993

*Australian copyright 1993
Philippine copyright 1993
This edition 1993*

ISBN 0 263 78260 3

*Set in 10 on 11½ pt Linotron Times
01-9310-53655*

*Typeset in Great Britain by Centracet, Cambridge
Made and printed in Great Britain*

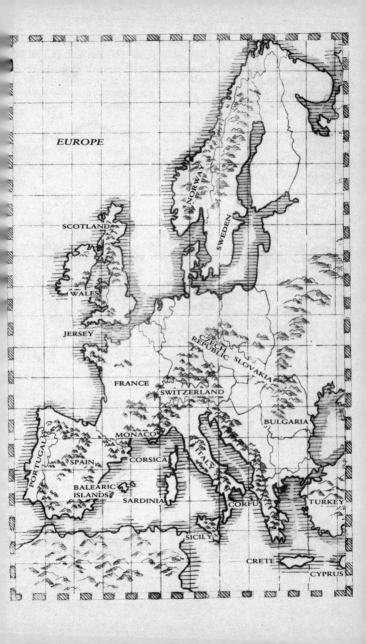

# CHAPTER ONE

'LIVE, damn you!' The furious words roared from somewhere away in the starlit, splashing darkness. '*You must live*!'

Wrapped in the velvety peace of near exhaustion, Mallory paid only the dreamiest attention. It might have been the night shouting at her, or the sea suddenly taking on a human voice.

But no, that was wrong. This warm Black Sea which would soon rock her to eternity, this kindly sea would never talk to her so roughly. Its voice would be gentle as its sloping beach, quiet as these little waves which played so sweetly with her long dark hair. Soon these innocent waves would wash right over her, cover her like the lightest, purest shroud, forever and forever. . .

'"Down at the bottom of the deep blue sea,"' she chanted once more, as she had a moment ago. 'Only it's the Black Sea, isn't it? "Down at the bottom of the deep Black Sea, Catching fishes for my tea, See them swimming one, two——"'

'How dare you do this?' The voice exploded right in her ear, while a living presence stirred the water about her with tiresome vitality. 'How *dare* you?'

'I'm not doing anything.' Mallory made a great effort to be polite to this intruder whose anger, though water-cooled, still pushed and dragged at the edges of her quiet. 'Nothing at all. . .'

She let the words, the thought, all thought, drift away from her. It didn't matter. All that mattered was floating here among the waves, at one with the sea and sky as

7

she had been since this great peace had descended on her. An arm like knotted iron had hooked itself under her shoulders, but she accepted that as she could accept everything now, quietly, without struggling.

'Nothing at all,' she repeated, floating with the arm. 'Only going away. Somewhere nicer. . .'

'*Nowhere* is nicer than Bulgaria in summer.'

The words rang among the little waves with absolute conviction. He sounded less angry now, but still too lively.

'To kill yourself at all is a sin against life. To kill yourself in June, in Bulgaria——' the arm gripped and directed her in the water '—that is worse than bad. It is also stupid.'

'You're Bulgarian, then?' Mallory floated tranquilly along with him, wrapped in her cloak of exhausted, uncaring calm. 'I like the way you talk. So musical. . .'

'We are musical people.' The arm stayed under her, firm with the confidence of this being who had taken charge of her. 'We have music in Bulgaria like God taught the angels.' He guided her through the star-sheened water. 'You will hear it.'

'Hearrr it.' Mallory repeated the words as he had spoken them, just for the pleasure of their lilting certainty. 'I will, won't I? From the bottom of the sea. . .'

'You will hear it in God's good air, as you should.'

'No, no, I've finished with the air.' She tried to shake her head, her sea-frond hair pulling and coiling against her neck. 'I belong to the sea now.'

'The sea does not wish to have you.'

'Yes, it does. It's taken me, hasn't it?' Mildly irritated with him for making her argue, she turned her eternity-heavy head towards him. 'I know it didn't want to at first. . . so shallow. Then it carried me out for miles. . .'

'A hundred metres, maybe a hundred and fifty,' he corrected her through the lapping, swishing darkness. 'And even then it would only reach your shoulders. Children play in it every day.' Indignation swelled once more in the deep voice. 'Are you not ashamed?'

'Don't talk to me like that,' she pleaded, feeling his heat invading and disturbing her cold distances. 'Stop! Let me go. . .'

But he wouldn't. That arm had gripped her tight now, and had clamped her to the length of an iron-hard, sea-chilled body. Before she could even start fighting, it had drawn her mercilessly upright, made her leave her beautiful floating nowhere and accept once more the gravity of the real world.

'Let me go!'

She flailed her newly heavy limbs in vain. His shoulders were strong and spare as girders, his chest hard as a shield.

Half blinded by her streaming hair, she shook her head and peered once more through the clumped-together strands. Still she could see very little, only up there, between her and the light-dusted universe, the black outline of a head. Its straight nose defied the stars; its obstinate hair had already thrown off the water to spring back where it meant to be, high against the world. Below that silhouetted head all was darkness, and in the darkness a knotted-iron arm, a steely body, dragged her back.

'You're h-hateful!' She felt the hot tears prick at her eyes. 'Why can't you just l-leave me al-lone?'

He didn't bother to answer, just went on controlling her with that one arm. His other hand, she saw, was raised above their heads to grip some kind of boat, a pale hull supporting an angular pattern of steel deck-rails. The rails loomed closer as he hoisted her towards them, lifting her to the deck.

Lifting her back into the world, to face the reality she had been running away from. Before she knew it she had managed an angry, convulsive jerk which freed her of that retaining arm and brought her head above deck-level. Another jerk, a scramble, and she was on board, clear of this man. She uncoiled triumphantly. . .

Pain rattled at the top of her head. The stars flared and circled in a mad dance, flickered, and went out.

And now she was floating again, only the sea had changed. It didn't feel wet any more, but dry and cosy as a blanket. It wasn't blue-silver either, but white-gold, and beside her swam a white-gold eagle-winged tiger.

'What are you doing here?' she murmured, trying to work out why it was wrong for a tiger to be swimming in the sea.

'Before I heard your little song,' it answered in a voice that was tiger-deep, tiger-fierce, yet for a tiger strangely human. 'I was trying peacefully to fish. . .'

'Fish! That's what you should be — a fish.'

'I give you fair warning, *devoika*. I am no fish.'

'Of course you aren't; you're a. . .' She opened her eyes, drawn by that same note of intensity which had so disturbed her in the water. 'Oh.'

The tiger who had swum with her now sat on the bunk opposite. And in this white cabin-light he really was white-gold, though the colours were far earthier than they had been a minute ago. The white towelling robe barely skimmed his thighs, and below it the long legs, carefully controlled in the narrow space of the gangway, were tanned dark gold.

So were the powerful forearms. Mallory stared at them, wondering which of them she had accepted beneath her in the water. She tossed round on the

pillow, then screwed up her eyes with pain and dragged
a hand to the top of her head.

'Yes, you should have a bruise. It will hurt for a
while,' the deep voice informed her from the other side
of the cabin. 'But it is not so bad as I feared. You did
not break the skin.'

'What happened?' she asked feebly through the red
haze of her closed eyelids.

'You hit the deck-rail. You have been unconscious
for. . .' a pause, presumably to check '. . .about five
minutes. But I think maybe it was weakness, as much as
the blow, which knocked you out.'

'Five minutes.' She compared the tiny fragment of
time with the eternity she had hoped for. 'Why on earth
can't you mind your own business?' she burst out
fretfully. 'Why did you have to come bothering me? I
was only swimming — I could have got back to shore
alone, any time I wanted to!'

'You could not!' The undercurrent of intensity was
still there in the deep voice, this time surfacing as angry
dogmatism. 'You were in great difficulty! You had
actually travelled part of the way towards drowning!'

'I *hadn't*! I'd been swimming quite happily for. . .oh,
hours!'

How long had it been? She saw her earlier self on the
other side of that endless swim, distant and hard-edged
as the image in a convex mirror. She'd had to be
cunning, to wait until Richard was in the shower before
she'd unpacked her bikini, put it on, and called to him
that she was going for a late swim in the pool.

'At this time of night?' His voice over the rush of the
shower had been surprised and disapproving.

She hadn't cared about that, not any more. She hadn't
even bothered to answer, had just pulled her beach-
robe from her suitcase, flung it about her, and gone

down to smile her way glassily through the hotel lobby.
After that it had been easy to dodge in the moonless
dark through the shadowy pines to the deserted
beach. . .

Mallory shivered, and drew the blanket close to shut
out the pain of memory reviving. The fine sand had
shifted between her toes, cool and unfeeling as the
world she was escaping from. She'd dropped the beach-
robe and not stopped to see where it fell, just continued
bikini-clad into the welcoming sea. At first it had only
lapped at her ankles, then at her knees, her thighs, and
at last it had been waist-high and she had been able to
swim.

She'd never been a strong swimmer. She'd never been
a strong anything—that had been part of her trouble—
and suddenly it became part of her release. The sea had
decided to take her, so she'd be done with the whole
dirty, miserable mess called life.

Presently time and space had blended into one, and
both had lost their power over her. That was when she'd
turned on her back and floated—and hadn't she done
something else? Hadn't she made one last, cleansing
gesture? It had involved an undoing of hooks, a wrig-
gling in the water, and after it she'd started to chant that
old childhood rhyme to celebrate her freedom and her
one-ness with the forgiving sea. . .

Mallory opened her eyes in horror to the unblinking
white cabin-light. Furtively, trying not to let the movement show under the ochre-gold blanket, she patted the
area of her too narrow hips, then of her too small
breasts.

Neither was covered by anything but blanket. So she
really had kicked away the protecting briefs and dis-
creetly padded bra of her bikini.

'Easy, *devoika*, easy.' Her companion must have

noted the movement, or judged by her face what she had just discovered. 'I have seen naked women before. . .'

'Not me.' She pulled the blanket up to her chin in a panic. 'Nobody's seen me like this since I grew up.'

'And will not again, until you wish it.'

'As if I ever would.'

She kept her head turned away, hating him more. Now to the great evil of making her live he'd added the small one of knowing of her embarrassing thinness, the unsexy body which went so oddly, so humiliatingly, so inconveniently with a face like hers.

Had he noticed her face? She turned back to him and tried to lift her aching head, but it was too heavy. She found herself staring instead at the easiest part of him to see from here, his long, deeply tanned legs.

They looked far too tense to be reassuring. She could see each perfectly tuned muscle working to keep the feet and knees together. Little waves slapped the fibre-glass hull, rocking the boat to and fro, yet still those knees stayed tight against each other and drawn to a high, uncomfortable angle. Was he hiding something?

Maybe he read her thoughts. 'You fear me?'

She moved her head a fraction, the nearest she could come to a nod. 'You're much stronger than I am.'

'But I have not hurt you.'

'You think not?' She managed an ironic croak of a laugh. 'But, even in the way you mean, you can only say, "not yet".'

'That is unfair, *morska devoika*.' A dark-tanned hand reached from somewhere beyond the legs to touch the edge of the gold-ochre blanket. 'Did I not put this over you?'

'Wasn't it all part of keeping me alive?'

'I could have warmed you another way. . .'

'Don't!' She shuddered, and the hand removed itself.

'I think we talk of other things.' The deep voice was very low now, and very soft.

Too soft, Mallory thought in weak confusion. It was soft like the white ash when a wood fire burned low, and underneath it was still scorching hot.

'You were telling me,' the soft, hot voice continued a little too quickly, 'how you swam for many hours — at least, as it seemed to you. And then?'

'What? Oh. Well——' she blinked, trying to focus her weary thoughts ' — I floated, didn't I?'

'Floated and sang and were happy, till I spoilt it for you.' The voice hardened with an anger which would not be contained. 'Is that not so?'

'Yes.' She realised with surprise that he had got it exactly right. 'I was fine till you came along!'

'You were not fine!'

'I was, I was!' She felt new tears starting, and sniffled them back. 'You don't know. . .'

'It is you who do not know. Can you not feel how near to death by drowning you had come?' The hard-edged words pounded on. 'The water was beginning to lull you. . .'

'You're making it up,' she said, feebly furious in her turn. 'Even if there had been something like that happening, someone else would have come along eventually!' She had to let this arrogant man know that he was not a godlike figure in charge of the air, earth *and* sea!

'You *think* so?'

'I *know* so!'

He shrugged those powerful shoulders. 'But still I have not spoken of the worst!' That soft white-hot voice would brook no argument. 'The worst would be the loneliness.'

'Loneliness!' She flung the word back at him with all her scant force. 'Do you think I don't know about that?'

'Not like that. Your last moments on earth and no earthly soul to comfort you.'

Was it pity she could hear in the deep voice? If so, he could keep it. She wanted none of it, nor of his arguments either, though they were easily answered.

'And what do you know of loneliness?'

'Do not speak so, *devoika*.' The heat glowed again in the vibrant tones, sharpening the reprimand. 'Simply be thankful that you're still alive.'

'Thank you very much,' she murmured through a huge, ever growing weight of fatigue. 'Still alive, but still all alone.'

'That cannot be so,' the deep, soft voice returned, dogmatic as ever. 'Nobody has nobody.'

'Well, that's what I've got. Nobody.' She stared at the cabin's white ceiling, thinking of her divorced parents, who were as bad as nobody, and Richard, who had turned out to be worse.

'Nobody and nothing.'

'That is not true, *morska devoika*.' There he went again, unquestioningly sure that his view was the only right one. 'Such beauty as yours is not nothing. It is a very great something.'

'You like it then.' She wasn't asking a question but drearily stating a fact.

He noticed the dreariness at once. 'You are displeased that I speak of it?'

'It's only that I'm. . .' She frowned, wishing the thudding in her head didn't make it so hard for her to think straight. 'I'm not like that at all, not really. Well,' she reasoned behind her closed eyelids, 'you saw for yourself, didn't you?'

'I did?' He sounded puzzled. 'You think you are

beautiful only on the outside? And that I should have seen this?'

'I meant that I'm not beautiful at all,' she corrected him with weak impatience. 'Not really. You must have seen that before you covered me.'

'I did not. . .but we talk of other things.' The words followed each other too fast. 'You say that you have nobody and nothing. Were you then born of the sea-foam?'

'Hmm? What?'

Dazed by self-reproach, Mallory had barely heard the question. Was she mad, to have reminded him of her nakedness? And for what? Only to make the point that her inadequate, unfeminine body didn't match her sensual mouth and dark, tilted eyes. And to judge from the hurried way he'd backed off, he'd already noticed that for himself.

'Were you, then, sea-born,' he rephrased the question impatiently, 'like the goddess of love?'

'But that's just what I was trying to tell you!' She seized at the chance to explain. 'I'm no love-goddess; I just sometimes make men think that way. Some men.'

And always of a certain kind. If a man liked to wear flashy clothes and drop big names, to eat in better places than he could afford and run a car that turned heads in the street, then sure as sunrise he would home in on little Mallory. They seemed to have a nose for her, a sixth sense that sought her out even when they couldn't see her.

And once they got her they hadn't the least idea what to do with her. In public they would show her off like designer jewellery, and in private jump on her as she feared this man might, and have to be fought off.

Oh, how tired she was of fighting them off! That was one reason why Richard had seemed so attractive, rescuing her from that horrible party where the other men had all leered and grabbed and boasted how big they meant to be one day in show business. He'd never grabbed, not once in the month they'd been seeing each other. Instead he'd talked, and listened, and tried to understand. Or so it had seemed. . .

'Hmm?' She realised that her companion, the arrogant wretch who had dragged her back to life was now waiting to hear from her. 'I'm sorry,' she murmured, slurred with fatigue, 'were you asking me something?'

'I said,' he repeated with long-suffering distinctness, 'that we do not speak of love, but of belonging. You must belong somewhere.'

'To the sea.' Behind her closed eyelids, she could still see him. 'I told you when we were out there in the water.'

'You told me nonsense, *devoika*. A woman does not live in water.' He paused, then went on with new resolution. 'We will try another way. I know that you are English. . .'

'So you do.' She realised for the first time that he had spoken her own language from the start. 'How did you find out?'

'I have already said. It was your English song which led me to you.'

'And I was so sure I was miles from anywhere.' She sighed.

'So you have a country.' He kept doggedly to his line of questioning. 'You must also have a reason for being here in Bulgaria?' The probing voice, so soft and yet so determined, demanded an answer.

'Not now I haven't.'

She hadn't really meant to fob him off; she was just too tired to think about it. Too tired, and too unhappy.

They would take a spring break, Richard had promised. They would have a week, a whole week in a distant, romantic land where they knew nobody and nobody knew them.

Yes, she thought with bitter hindsight, it would have to be in a place where he wasn't known, wouldn't it?

'And there,' he'd told her, kissing her goodnight as he always did at the street door of her father's flat, 'we'll be together at last. Really together.'

And she had nestled in his tweedy arms, happy that he thought her worth waiting for. And so was he, or so it had seemed. She'd thought him well worth her long wait, this countryman lover who'd come to London only at weekends, and took her only to the quietest places, and never wanted to show her off at all.

No, he wouldn't want to do that, would he? Being seen with her was the last thing he'd want to risk.

But she'd been far too happy to think of anything like that. At last she'd had someone to live for, someone to care about who cared about her. The idea of being with him, man and woman joined in love, had given meaning to her whole shapeless, unsatisfactory life. With that closeness to look forward to, she'd understood why she'd always held back till now.

Of course she'd held back. Those first steps in physical love must be with the right man, and with the right man only. . .

But her precious right man had turned out to be a vile cheat.

Why, why had she returned her father's call at once, as his urgent phone message had commanded? She needn't have. They'd only just arrived at the hotel, their flight delayed by something or other explained on the intercom when she had been too besotted with happiness to listen. She could have left that call till morning, and gone straight to bed with Richard as they'd planned. That way, she'd have had at least one night. . .

In a fool's paradise. Her father might be a hopeless parent, might forget her birthday and stay out all hours and smell of whisky at breakfast, might provoke her over and over again to ask why he and his now divorced wife had ever adopted her, but he was a good policeman. As he'd pointed out to her on the phone, he'd never have reached the rank of detective inspector without having a nose for a villain.

'And this one,' he'd stated unanswerably, 'is leading my daughter up the garden path. He's married, with three kids.'

'He can't be.' She'd leant against the wall of the little phone booth in the hotel lobby, feeling sick.

'His wife's name is Christine. The children are Polly, Charlotte, and one still in arms called Adam. . .'

'You've got the wrong man. This is Richard Sherwood, from Upper Barton near Trowbridge ——'

'There isn't any such place,' Simon Hawthorne had cut in with devastating professional certainty. 'Though he's used that address before.'

'When?' she'd demanded, knowing too well that he would give her chapter and verse.

'Last year, in the Seabrook Hotel, Kensington.' Here it came. 'I don't know who the woman was, but he signed her in as Mrs Sherwood.'

'Maybe she *was* Mrs Sherwood,' Mallory suggested wildly, hardly noticing how she'd been forced to admit there might be one.

'Couldn't have been,' the solid, coldly reasoning voice had continued at the London end of the line. 'Christine Sherwood was in hospital at the time, having Adam.'

'Oh, God!'

It all fitted so well. The obscure meeting-places, the letter returned by the Post Office, Richard's refusal to give a phone number. He'd said that a busy farmer wasn't around phones much, and instead had rung her at odd times like midnight and dawn. One of his calls, late in the evening, had ended abruptly in the middle of something, she'd been saying. She'd thought they'd been cut off, and had waited for him to ring again, but he hadn't. Now it seemed only too clear that his wife must have come back unexpectedly early from where-ever she'd been for that evening. . .

'No good hanging about having hysterics.' That was her father, brisk as if he were dealing with one of his constables. 'Get yourself together, and come back home.'

'Home?' she'd asked with false lightness. 'Where's that?'

'Don't get clever with me, girl,' he'd rapped back down the line as she'd known he would. 'I want you out of there on the first plane that'll take you.'

'And you'll meet me off it?' she asked pointedly.

The point found its mark. 'You know I can't do that.' A pause. 'Shall I try and get hold of your mother?'

'In Norwich? What can she do from there?'

'Maybe talk to you. . .'

'She'll be out on a case.' Mallory thought of the years she had lived with her busy GP mother, whose every waking thought was for her patients. 'She's always out on a case.'

'Damn career women,' Simon Hawthorne had grum-bled. 'Look, Mal, I can see you day after tomorrow. . .'

Mal. Shortened like that it was Latin for 'evil', and her full name meant 'unlucky'. She'd told him so after she'd found it in a book of surnames, but he'd shrugged, said her mother had chosen it, and still called her Mal.

Even when she was little he'd never addressed her as, say, 'honey-bunch', or 'tuppence', the sweet, nonsensical names other men gave their daughters. He never even called her 'love'. Just 'girl', or 'Mal'.

'I'm talking to you, girl.' There he went, worried only that she didn't pay him proper respect. 'You've got to leave that scum right now, do you hear?'

'Yes, Father,' she'd responded. 'I'll do that.'

She stirred her aching limbs. What was that he was saying? Her father's voice was still echoing in her head. This one was different, deeper and more resonant, but, now that she thought of it, she could hear the same lord-of-creation overtones.

'Someone ashore will be worrying about you.'

'You think so?' She turned her head towards the wave-lapped hull, suddenly tired to death.

'You will sleep soon, *devoika*. But first you must tell me who you are.'

'You're not asking much, are you?' She heard a rattling, mirthless noise, and realised she had meant it as a laugh. 'How do I know who I am? I don't know anything about myself.'

'That cannot be so. You must know something.'

But Mallory had almost drifted off. Somewhere far away, ten years away, her adoptive mother was still answering her questions about it.

'Hormonal imbalance brought on by the menopause. . .'

The dry, medical phrases didn't sanitise the story. Mallory had simply translated them.

'You mean my mother was a middle-aged nymphomaniac.'

'Don't be too hard on her, my dear. After you were born it all settled down again, and her husband ——'

'She had a husband?'

'A husband, but no other children.' Linda Hawthorne had always believed in giving the facts straight. 'He took her back, but he wouldn't have you, the baby. Our good luck.'

'Thanks for that, Ma.'

Mallory had wanted to hug her mother for those compassionate words, but somehow Dr Hawthorne always generated her own professional distance, even from those closest to her. So instead Mallory had gone on with her questioning.

'And my father?'

'A. . .a seaman.' Even Dr Hawthorne had faltered on that one. 'And he. . .he couldn't speak English.'

'She didn't teach him?'

'They. . .they weren't together long enough.'

'A one-night stand,' Mallory burst out bitterly. 'And she never even found out which country he came from.'

She'd been fifteen then. At eighteen, encouraged by her mother and armed with all of the few facts that were known, she'd travelled to Southampton to find the woman who'd given birth to her. But all she'd found was a name in a book of remembrance.

'But I don't remember anything.' She didn't know she'd spoken the words aloud until she heard her own voice over the swimming haze in her head. 'Nothing at all. . .'

'Nothing?' the deep voice queried, startling her awake and back to the present. 'Nothing at all?'

'Not about that.' She tried to gather her wits. 'Not about anything that matters.'

'Your name, for instance?'

'It means evil, or unlucky.'

'You are wandering, *devoika*.' He sounded anxious. 'Perhaps you hit your head worse than I thought.'

'Perhaps I did.'

For no reason that she could understand, his anxiety was strangely welcome to her. She wanted more of it. She wanted enough of it to float her away as the sea had floated her, to wrap around her as this blanket wrapped her, to shoulder her troubles and make light of them as he had made light of her body when he'd lifted it from the water.

But if she told him her troubles he would make her go back to them. They all would. The bank would want her back in Securities, training with endless dark-clad men who cared nothing for her even when they were on the make, and women who never seemed to have any time for her. Her father would want her back in the flat, crossing his path one day in three if she was lucky. Even Richard would want to know where she was, to be reassured. . .

Let him worry, Mallory thought. Let them all worry. I'll go back to them when I'm good and ready, and not a minute before.

'When I first met you,' her companion was saying, 'you were singing a silly rhyme about fishes at the bottom of the sea. Do you remember that?'

Slowly, deliberately, knowing exactly what she was doing, Mallory shook her aching head. It jumped and rang with the movement, but perhaps that was only right. It almost helped, to know that she was punished at once for the lie.

'So you remember nothing,' he said at last. 'Not even your name, only some silly meaning which means nothing.'

'You've given me a new name.' She didn't have to act her sleep-drugged languor. '*De-voi-ka*,' she brought out, suprised that she could repeat it so exactly. 'What does it mean?'

'Only "girl". It is not a real name at all.'

'Girrl,' she repeated, liking the way he made it sound.

How strange to think it was the same word she heard so often in her father's brusque tones. Even in English it came out quite different in this man's lilting accent, almost like a caress.

And sometimes he'd added another word to it. What was that, now? If she opened her mind to it, perhaps it would come.

Sure enough, her tongue was already shaping it. '*Morr-ska de-voi-ka*.' She got it out with distant, sleepy satisfaction. 'You called me that, as well. What does it mean?'

'Sea-girl. Mermaid. Something——' a hand descended to her still-wet hair, and pushed it away from her face ' — I never thought to catch when I set up my fishing-line.'

Out in the night, another boat chugged by. Its wake lifted their bright little cabin world and dropped it, lifted and dropped it, and various unseen things rattled. As the disturbance stilled and the alien noise died away in the distance, Mallory had a curious feeling of relief. She had escaped after all. Unseen forces were on the look-out for her, to drag her back to where she didn't want to be, but they didn't have to find her. She could still dodge them.

That warm hand was still there, light on her hair. Well clear of the bruise, it cradled her temple with a tenderness she felt she had never known before in her life.

'Can't I be your *mor-ska de-voi-ka*?' she whispered, barely moving her lips. 'Just for tonight?'

'Sleep, then, *morska devoika*,' it whispered back. 'For tonight, at least, I have you safe.'

# CHAPTER TWO

SOMETHING had changed. Or was it only the light which made it seem so, this piercing, uneven light which wavered and flickered against her closed eyelids like a candle-flame in the wind?

'Not a candle,' Mallory murmured to herself, eyes shut against that intrusive light. 'It's far too bright and hot and strong to be a candle.'

She turned over, and pulled the blanket up to her ears. That was better. Yet still the glimmering light worried at her senses, dragging her through the haze of half waking until she opened blurry eyes on smooth dark blue and fluffy sun-yellow—smooth berth cushions, a fluffy blanket and, before her clearing eyes, a curving expanse of pale blue fibreglass. . .

She shot up in the bunk, and wished she hadn't. For one thing, the movement dragged at her long hair and started an ache at the top of her head. For another, it slid the blanket down to her waist and left her small breasts helplessly exposed.

She covered herself with a furtive glance round. To her relief, the cabin was empty. Wavering, sea-flashing sunlight cascaded from four lengthened portholes over three dark blue berths like the one where she lay, all cleared to be used as seats. Mahogany woodwork glowed, kaleidoscope-patterned china shone from snug lockers, a stainless-steel sink blazed mirror-bright, and a trim cooker swung with the rocking of the waves, its blue-patterned kettle always upright. All was pin-neat, shining and deserted—so where was he, the man who had dragged her from the sea?

On deck, perhaps? 'H-hello?'

The timid piping of her own voice made her straighten with a long, unsteady breath. She must do better than that to be heard among the sea noises. It all sounded so busy up there beyond the louvred mahogany doors and closed mahogany hatch that he'd never hear her unless she made the effort.

'Hello?' she called, much louder. 'Where are you?'

No answer. She listened, and realised that the busy noises were only the soft wind playing about the mast among the ropes and stays. She could hear none of the solid, purposeful sounds a man would make, only the call of sea-birds and the lapping of waves.

And anyway, why had he closed the cabin, here at anchor on a beautiful morning? Careful not to jolt her aching head, she swung her feet to the cool mahogany floor, and listened again.

Still she could hear no human sound. Had he left her here alone? And if so, why?

She rose as smoothly as she could, and took up the blanket to wrap herself sarong-style. It was far too big and heavy to stay up without being held, and it hampered all her movements, but she wasn't going far. Even with her short stride, she needed a mere step to push one-handed at the double cabin doors.

They wouldn't be pushed.

All she achieved was to swivel the louvred slats to let in bars of sunlight and glimpses of a sunny, deserted cockpit. She tried with both hands, and the blanket slid down at once from her breasts. She pulled it hastily back, though almost convinced she was alone, and held it round herself as she pushed again at the doors. Only when they refused to give did she forget all modesty, raise both arms over her head, and tug at the hatch with growing outrage. The blanket fell unheeded to her waist, her hips, her knees, and at last settled to the polished floor, to be kicked aside when she whirled to survey the cabin.

How dared he? Careless of her aching head, she stepped forwards naked and unhampered, her long hair swishing about her like the tail of an angry cat as she tried the fore-hatch.

It wouldn't budge.

What did he mean to do—kidnap her? And anyway, where had he gone? Was it for this that he'd pulled her from the water, to leave her alone at sea in a boat she hadn't the remotest idea how to sail? Not that all the sailing know-how in the world would have helped her now, locked in like a child who'd been naughty.

'Don't panic, girl,' she told herself in her father's tones. 'There's always another way, if you can find it.'

Cautious this time for the ever threatening headache, she lowered herself to one of the empty berths. A glance through the porthole showed the boat was not nearly as far out as she would have imagined. Over the water's placid blue-green she could see tiny umbrellas along gold-white sand, and gentle, pine-clad slopes scattered with peach-coloured roofs over arched white walls.

So that was Duni, the place Richard had chosen with such care. The dream holiday-place, made for lovers. . .

'I won't go back there, I *won't*,' she burst out into the wave-lapped, wind-blown quiet. 'I won't ever talk to Richard again. I won't even *see* him.'

Which was all very well, but what did she do instead? Find a way out of there somehow, and finish what she'd inadvertently begun last night? Let the sea take her?

'No!'

The word seemed torn from her without her will. She

shot to her feet, and had to clutch at her throbbing
head.

'That's what I'll do,' she announced to the sunny,
uncaring air. 'I'll find some aspirin.'

Would her host, her captor, keep aspirin? She
couldn't imagine him needing them, the mysterious
creature who had dragged her out of the night and who
now had vanished with the morning. She cast back over
her memories of him. First there'd been an angry voice,
then a ruthlessly strong frame, and then. . .

Then what? Try as she might, she couldn't conjure up
any clear, full picture of the man. There'd been that
black profile, the nose blade-straight against the stars,
the hair defiantly upright under the weight of the sea-
water. Then there'd been electric light, white and flat
from the ceiling, and two dark-tanned, springy legs,
tensed over arched feet as if. . .

As if he'd needed to hide something. Only it had been
all right; he'd pushed her hair away from her face, and
she'd. . .

'I slept!' Mallory exclaimed in wonder.

How could she possibly have slept? Why, the very
thought now of that warm hand at her temple, those
gentle fingers in her damp hair, sent shivers down her
spine.

'Aspirin! Aspirin, aspirin, aspirin. . .'

Intoning the word like a spell against something or
other, she wrenched at the drawers. They held stainless-
steel cutlery, tools, charts, a compass, pencils. The last
had documents in Bulgarian script, and a New York
postcard written in a flowing feminine hand. Mallory
picked it up to read the address, but instead found her
eyes straying to its message.

'Congratulate us, darling. . .'

Ashamed, she closed it away and knelt to the cupboards. 'Aspirin, aspirin, aspirin. . .'

The first turned out to be a refrigerator. The second had butter in a ceramic dish, and a heel of bread, and apricot jam—why hadn't she noticed how hungry she was? She licked her lips and went on searching. The lower shelf had stainless-steel saucepans that clashed and clattered against each other. She ignored her renewed headache and moved them aside to see what lay behind them.

'Aspirin, aspirin. . .'

'You will find them——' the deep voice was ominously husky '—in the locker futher forward.'

Still kneeling, Mallory turned in horror, hair flying and settling down her back. Then she sprang to her feet and flung her arms across her body in the age-old, protective attitude of a woman surprised naked.

'I. . . I didn't hear you.' She stared accusingly at the louvred doors, wide now to the cloudless sky.

He swung down into the cabin. 'My dinghy is inflatable, very quiet. And you make much noise.'

'Wh-where've you been?' she demanded weakly. 'I've been up for ages.'

'I, too.'

But he almost whispered it, as if he meant something quite different. With a sick feeling of defencelessness, she summoned all her courage to try to make her eyes meet his. They would go no further than his narrow waist, which was belted into jeans that caressed every line of his supple thighs.

'Did I not warn you, *devoika*, that I am no fish?'

'Warn me?' She forgot her headache in a blush so furious that she could feel it in the nape of her neck, her shoulders, even her breasts. 'You talk as if I were here on purpose!'

'We do not talk of purpose, or of will, or of reason.' The words came out choked, yet controlled. 'It is not reasonable, what happens to us at this moment.'

'Nothing's happening to me!'

'You say not?' he demanded softly.

She stood dumb. She couldn't remember ever having seen his eyes, didn't know anything about them, yet she knew where they looked as they spoke. They affected her like a touch, the gentlest and most direct of touches on the coral peak of the breast which, for all her efforts, had stayed uncovered by her arm.

'But no, you know better than that,' he went on with maddening, matter-of-fact arrogance. 'Your body speaks as clear to you as mine does to me.'

'This is impossible! Give me that blanket.' She lunged towards him, intent on the gold-ochre folds round his feet.

It was the worst thing she could have done. He didn't even need to reach out for her, only to set his hands either side of her waist and raise her to face him.

Still she wouldn't meet his eyes. Instead she instinctively closed her mouth, and breathed in hard through her nose.

'Wh-what's that aftershave?' she asked, desperately casual.

'Aftershave!' he repeated contemptuously. 'This —' he plucked at the black cotton of his T-shirt and released another waft of spicy fragrance ' — comes from some mixture of dead flowers that my — ' he stopped, and changed what he had meant to say ' — that is all over my cupboards. I must clean it out.'

'But — but it's a nice smell. C-cinnamon,' she gabbled as if her soul depended on identifying the contents of the pot-pourri or whatever it was. 'And other spices. And roses. . .'

'Dead roses. We——' his fingers cupped her chin, gently forcing her head upwards '——are alive.'

'Y-yes.' She kept her lashes down. 'I'm alive, thanks to you, and I'm——' surely this would distract them both '——I'm grateful. It's amazing how the daylight makes everything——'

'Look at me, *devoika*.'

And so, reluctuntly, she saw his eyes at last.

'Why, they're like your voice,' she murmured. 'They burn——'

'Quiet, *devoika*.'

His lips, too, burnt as they touched hers. For a long moment they stayed like that, his gentle hands on her waist and his mouth on hers. Then he was no longer content to taste, but had to hold and savour and demand more. She gave more, gave it with a willingness that shamed her. She couldn't help it, couldn't stop her tongue seeking his, or her thighs surging blindly to the animal satisfaction her mind shudderingly rejected.

His mouth released hers, and traced a fiery track over her cheek, her ear, her neck. His hands moved downwards over her, raising dark, physical sparks which fanned out and exploded in detestable sweetness until she thought her enclosed, imprisoned body would melt with longing.

Only when he approached the centre of that longing did she manage to gasp out in protest.

'Please don't! Nobody's ever touched me there.'

His hands stilled, and his lips at her shoulder. 'You are virgin?' His breath whispered over her skin. 'You, who are made for love?'

She tried to drag herself away from him, but couldn't. 'I. . .never wanted the first time to be. . .like this.' She took a ragged breath, and forced out more. 'With a man I don't. . .know well enough. . .to trust.'

'I will take care of you.' His lips moved unbearably against her shoulder. 'I promise.'

'And if. . .' She summoned all her strength for the clear, cold argument she needed. 'If I have a baby?'

It worked. For a moment their bodies froze, linked in the heat of desire. She had to fight the urge to fling her arms round his neck, give herself up to that miserable, treacherous sweetness and let tomorrow take care of itself.

But already he had broken away from her. Slowly, slowly before her lowered gaze, his denim-covered knees flexed with easy grace, and his tanned, powerful arm stretched down to lift the blanket. Well-kept hands shook and spread it, and then the taut, belted jeans disapppeared behind a wall of gold-ochre wool.

'For the love of heaven——' the order came out breathless and irresistibly urgent ' — turn round!'

She obeyed, and felt the fluffy gold-ochre folds drop to her shoulders. His fingers brushed her neck, sending excitement sparking anew into her scalp and along her spine, but he was only freeing her hair. Already he had stepped away from her.

'Why do you do this to me?' he demanded over the distance he had put between them. 'Am I made of stone, that I should have to keep from you? Are you not ashamed?'

'*Me* ashamed?' She clutched the blanket about her and whirled to face him, angry enough to ignore the achc which rushed back to the top of her head. 'It wasn't my idea to be left here all by myself. *Locked in*!' she added, newly furious. 'What did you think you were doing?'

'And if I had left you free to throw yourself again into the sea?' Dark eyes blazed into hers. 'If you had chosen to take your life while I was not there to stop you?'

'I told you! I wasn't trying to take my life — I just swam out too far!'

'Hmm. . .well, I locked you in, *devoika*,' his sober tone made it the only sensible thing to do, 'because I did not wish to risk that I come back here and find you gone.'

'Come back from *where*?'

She winced, and eased a hand from the woollen folds to her head. It was a relief to close her eyes. Somehow not to see him, not to see anything at all, felt safer as well as less painful.

'Where've you *been* all this time?' She hated the weak note of complaint in her own voice, but could do nothing to check it.'

He ignored the question. 'Sit down. I must pass you.'

'What?' Safe inside her blanket and the throbbing haze of her own head, she held her ground. 'What do you mean?'

'You block my way,' the deep voice informed her. 'There is little space here, and I do not wish to be close to you.'

'I haven't the plague, you know,' she dared to point out, hazily indignant. 'I won't suddenly explode —'

'No, but *I* might,' he cut in fiercely. 'You are covered now, and your breasts no longer speak to me. . .'

'They never did.' Her eyes flew open to glare into his. 'You imagined it.'

'You wish me to prove it?' He reached for the blanket, ready to grasp it. 'You wish me to make them speak again?'

'No!' She sank on suddenly weak knees to the berth nearest to her and furthest from him. 'But only,' she added from this new, safe distance, 'because you're a beastly great *bully*!'

'And you are unfair as only a woman can be.'

But already some of the heat had gone from his voice. Having won his argument by brute force, he sauntered past her to the narrower part of the boat, and pulled down a cupboard door which stayed horizontal to form a shelf.

Memory stabbed at her as she noted the straight, defiant profile. Yes, this was how she'd seen him last night against the stars. The morning brightness showed more detail, like red-brown glints where the black hair had caught the sun, and straight black eyebrows, and long black lashes. His complexion was not so much tanned as weathered, to ivory-gold at the temples, to copper-gold over the cheeks, and to teak-gold on the thrusting nose which would always take the full force of wind and sun.

He was, she realised with dismay, strikingly handsome. From high forehead to assertive nose to square jaw, from poised head to wide shoulders to long, springy legs, he was built on a grand scale. The cabin, which until he arrived had seemed roomy enough, was now bursting with him. If he tried to stand to his full height, he'd go right through the ceiling.

'No wonder you're so arrogant,' she murmured resentfully.

'Please?' The fine head tilted, listening.

'Nothing.'

Women must turn in the street to stare after him. Staring at him herself, taking in each vigorous, graceful movement as he searched through the cupboard, she had the strangest feeling that she'd seen it happen. Yes, surely she'd actually *seen* him with eager women flocking about him in light summer dresses?

I'm dreaming, Mallory told herself.

'Your aspirin.' He had shaken two from the bottle into his hand, and now laid them on the edge of the galley where she could reach. 'Take,' he commanded, and filled a French toughened glass with water.

Mallory gratefully obeyed. By the time he lowered the glass to her, powerful fingers well back from her own cautious hand, she had swallowed the first white tablet. She took the next, finished the water, and looked up in embarrassment as her stomach gurgled.

'So you are also hungry.' He had lifted a berth cushion and removed the mahogany panel below it, to haul out a green sports bag. 'Well, I will feed you. But not till I have clothed you.'

She slammed the empty glass to the galley-top. 'I'm not a poor little orphan. . .'

'Take.' He thrust something at her. 'And wear.'

She wanted to throw it back at him, but she had to wear something. She accepted it grudgingly, and felt her eyes widen as the exotic garment unfolded in her hands.

'Th-thank you.' She glanced at his austere black T-shirt, then examined the vivid rose-russet shirt he had given her. 'You really mean me to wear this? Why, it's —'

'It is a bad, useless thing.'

'Which makes it just right for me?' she flashed, hurt and bewildered.

'For you?' The long lashes swept down and up, leaving the dark eyes more composed. 'Excuse me.' He sketched a brief bow. 'I did not think of what I was saying.'

'Er — that's all right,' she answered wonderingly.

Had he really apologised to her? The more she thought of it the more astonished she felt, as if the sea itself had suddenly confessed to human error.

'But still I have no use for this red shirt,' he added. 'It would be wrong to throw it away new, so I bring it here to wear out quickly. Now *you* —' the strong lips curved in a brief, devastating smile ' — can wear it for me.'

'Glad to be of service.'

She meant it ironically, but couldn't stop her own mouth relaxing and responding to that smile. His teeth were as perfect as the rest of him, a white flash in the well-proportioned jaw. To distract herself, she stroked the autumn-bright, abstract patterns on the shirt's high collar.

'This is hand embroidery, isn't it? Is it Bulgarian national costume or something?'

'Certainly not.' Frosty once more, he moved past her to the partly open hatch. 'It is a costume only for —' the contempt returned to his tone as he sought an idea trivial enough for the unlucky shirt ' — for operetta. For a gypsy fiddler in a café.'

He took the three steps to the deck in a single, triumphant swing, and looked back with a hand on each door. 'A gypsy fiddler in a café,' he repeated with relish. 'I wish I had said that when she gave it to me. . .'

'Sh-she?'

The minute the timid interruption was out, Mallory cursed herself. There had to be a woman, many women, in his life, and who but a woman would have given him this shirt? Nor was it any of her business, yet still she waited, breathless, to hear about the particular woman who could make him speak with such feeling.

'But I held my peace,' he went on, rebuking the interruption, 'and made as if I liked it.'

His vehemence told her all she needed to know. Only a woman very close, very dear could have affected him so strongly. To mask the new, leaden misery inside her, she spurred herself to anger.

'You're talking about your wife, aren't you?'

'I am.' He spat out the words as if they hurt his tongue.

They certainly hurt Mallory, in a way all too sickeningly familiar. Two married men in a row, her chaotic thoughts threw at her, two cheats, two bastards one after the other.

'You. . .you made love to me.' She dropped the beautiful shirt, which had somehow become unclean, and huddled into her blanket. 'A married man.'

She stared at him, hoping he would deny it, but he didn't. Instead he jerked his head back, then brought it forwards in a strange, vigorous nod, dark eyes narrowed between straight eyebrows and straight mouth.

'No longer.'

'What?' she stared at him, more bewildered than ever. 'Are you telling me you *aren't* married?'

'I am not married, no.' The dark eyes mocked hers while he repeated that strange back-then-forward nod. 'Does that make you feel better?'

'M-marriage vows are important,' she protested weakly.

'They are, *devoika*,' he answered on a sigh. 'They are.'

'Then you're divorced?' She felt small, and mean, and prying, but she had to know.

Perhaps he understood the conflict within her. The dark gaze softened, and he shook his head in another strange gesture which looked like *no*, but must surely mean *yes*.

It did. 'I am divorced, yes. Already she has married her rat-man——' the contempt was back in full force ' —who she obviously thought a better prospect than me.'

'She l-left you for someone else?' Mallory wondered how any woman could do such a thing.

'Have I not said so?' Again he shook his head in that

side-to-side yes, dark eyes stormy. 'In that drawer——'
he indicated it '—you will find her postcard, telling me
of her new husband.'

'The one from New York that starts "Congratulate
us". . .?' Mallory broke off in confusion. 'That's all I
read, honest.'

'A postcard——' he cut her short with a splendid
shrug '—is for all the world to see. And now, we talk of
other things.' His tone made it clear he meant to choose
which things. 'Still you wear no clothes, *devoika*.'

'Oh.' She pulled her blanket closer, and stooped to
retrieve the dropped shirt. 'I'd better put this on, hadn't
I?' For some reason she felt suddenly full of optimism
and high spirits, as if the faithful Black Sea sun had
hidden for a few minutes and now shone again. 'Why do
you nod for no, and shake your head for yes?' she
demanded idly, unbuttoning the shirt.

'All Bulgarians do this. Did you not know?' He
sounded impatient. 'In the West I learn the other way,
but now I am home I do it our way.'

'Your way. That's——' on impulse she turned to him,
and copied his nodding no '—like this, isn't it?'

Whatever's got into me? she wondered as she felt her
hair settle down again to her blanket-covered shoulders,
and heard his short intake of breath. I *never* flirt, not
anywhere, let alone when it's this dangerous.

But still she fluttered her lashes and let her glance
challenge his.

'Stop that!' His eyes bit like fire, his voice like frost.
'You are being unfair again, *devoika*.'

Unfair, and foolish too. She knew it, yet had to go on
to try copying his head-shaking yes. Her widened gaze
stayed locked with his, dancing and teasing in a way
which made her cringe inwardly, though she couldn't
seem to stop.

'You wish me to make love to you?' he demanded with brutal directness. 'Remember I, too, have no way to hold him back, this child you do not wish to have.'

'It isn't only that.' Chilled back to good sense, she felt her mouth set into its usual defensive severity. 'It's ——'

'That you do not know me well enough to trust,' he threw harshly back at her. 'And I agree. But if I treat you as a decent woman, *devoika*, then you must act like one.'

'All right, all right,' she snapped, guilty yet rebellious. 'You can stop preaching now.'

'Preaching!' His roar echoed round the fibreglass walls. 'Do not try me too far, *devoika*.'

'Right!' She turned her back on him. 'So why don't you go away, and let me ——'

The cabin doors banged shut before she could finish. She flung the shirt about her, and was soothed at once by its ghosts of cinnamon and of roses, the pot-pourri he'd so scornfully called 'dead flowers'. Was it his ex-wife who had scattered it in his wardrobe? Mallory wondered again about the woman who could inspire such bitterness.

Whoever she was, she had a rare and daring clothes sense. This shirt must have been specially made, specially designed even, to stay so sturdily masculine in spite of its embroidery and its glowing, subtle colours. The severely cut heavy silk would go one way only — its own way.

Like his hair, she thought, and hurriedly rolled the oversize sleeves to shoulders loose as a caftan on her own slight frame.

The hem settled at her knees, so at least she needn't borrow his trousers. Trying to imagine belting herself into his trousers, and rolling up the legs so she could walk about in them, she took refuge in a brief giggle.

He must have heard it through the closed door. 'You have finished? Good.' He opened the doors. 'Now we eat. . .'

He stopped, sooty lashes sweeping down over the ember-dark eyes. Then he swallowed hard, and reached for something outside the cabin.

'Catch!'

'Right.' She found herself holding some minor piece of sailing gear — a length of strong elastic cord bound in yellow and brown woven cloth with a hook at either end. 'Er — thank you.'

She put it round her waist as he intended. But when she had closed the two brown hooks on the rose-russet silk, she heard a brief, exasperated sigh.

'And after all,' he told her, 'it does not help much.'

'Doesn't help what?'

But she only needed to glance at him to see what. Dismayed, she peered down at the silk which covered her from neck to knees.

'You can't see through it or anything?'

'I can *remember* through it. . . Never mind.' He pushed her almost roughly aside, and made for the galley. 'Now we eat.'

'Can I help?'

'Only by waiting on deck ——' he took two brown, kaleidescope-patterned plates from their locker, and set them with too much care on the galley ' — out of my way.'

Shrugging, she mounted the three steps from the cabin, and felt her spirits lift as she entered the wide blue morning. The sun was well up, and ashore the day's pleasure had begun. The tiny fringed umbrellas had unfurled, sunbathers lay on the sand, swimmers played in the shallow inshore waters, and a little further out the occasional windsurfer glided by on butterfly sails.

One of those could have been me, she reflected, if I hadn't returned my father's call. One of them could still be Richard. . .

But no, of course it couldn't. Whatever Richard had done when he'd found her missing, he couldn't continue his holiday as if nothing had happened. That, she realised with a new, shaming insight, had been the whole idea when she'd run away last night.

I wanted to hurt him, she admitted to herself, and ruin his holiday. She'd had no clear idea of what she'd intended to do when she'd stepped into the sea all those hours ago. She'd just wanted to get away from Richard to punish him for his treachery. . . Perhaps she could simply hide in the water until he'd tired of looking for her, or perhaps she would swim for a while, then return to the hotel and book into another room. *Whatever* she'd intended, it certainly hadn't been to kill herself. But she had got into difficulties, so no wonder he was so angry, the man who had rescued her from her own foolishness.

What would be happening now, there on the shore? Richard would have reported her missing. Already her passport-photo might be enlarged for a poster, and search-parties might be out looking for her. All that trouble she was causing, and would go on causing, because she wasn't going back; she just wasn't. . .

'Fruit juice.'

He handed it up from the cabin in a brimming glass. Newly humbled, she thanked him with real gratitude.

'It is made from peaches,' he told her. 'Is it not good?'

'Delicious.'

Surprised at her own thirst, she drained the glass and offered it back. Instead of taking it, he refilled it from a waxed carton.

'We have this instead of coffee,' he explained, 'and

the rest of our breakfast is in there.' He nodded past her at a straw basket she hadn't noticed until now. 'Unpack it, please.'

How he did order one about. Still, perhaps it was worth it, for the contents of this basket. The round crusty loaf was warm from the oven, and went perfectly with the sliced hard sausage and the butter he had brought from the cabin. After it they had a cheese pastry he called a *banitsa*, then bright red cherries which he said he'd bought direct from the farmer who supplied fruit to the hotels.

'So this is why you disappeared?' she murmered, ever more comfortable as her empty stomach filled. 'To fetch breakfast.'

'Certain things must be fresh every day.' He rose, and returned to the cabin. 'Pass in the dishes, please. Good.' He set them in the sink. 'Now you may pack the rest of the food back into the basket, and hand it in to me.'

More orders, but she didn't mind. 'How tidy you are,' she commented idly.

'On a boat it is the only way.'

'Can I help?' she offered as she had earlier, and rose to her feet. 'I could soon learn where you keep things. . .'

'Stay there.' Hunkered down at the fridge to put away the butter, he turned his head towards her. 'And wait.'

She blinked, but didn't dare argue. Something in the terse command, a gravity in the set of his mouth, the almost menacing calm of the dark eyes made her return unquestioningly to her place on the bench.

Disturbed, she waited there with hands clutched together.

All through breakfast, I was having a sort of holiday from life, she realised with a flutter at the pit of her stomach. In fact, I've been doing that ever since I went to sleep here last night.

Now came the reckoning. For a brief, blessed time, while they'd eaten, she had forgotten the hue and cry she must have caused ashore. The minute he'd landed he must have heard about the Englishwoman who late last night had left her hotel room and not been seen again. For some reason of his own he hadn't mentioned it yet, but he was going to now, the minute he'd finished what he was doing and rejoined her on deck.

'Well, I won't go back,' she whispered, stiff with resolution. 'Not to the way things were. I'll make a new start, somewhere outside England. . .'

She closed her mouth hurriedly as the tall figure mounted with easy grace from the cabin. That was just what she needed — to be found talking to herself.

If he'd heard her, he gave no sign of it. Still sombre, he sat on the opposite bench and stared past her to the ever more lively beach. Then he sighed, his full mouth lengthening, his straight eyebrows drawing together, until at last he turned to her with all of his fine features set in straight, determined lines.

Here it comes, Mallory thought. The real world catching up with me.

And the real world did, with a vengeance, and proved even more complicated and unyieldingly practical than she had feared.

'You must be wondering——' the dark eyes held hers with alert, enquiring attention ' — what the police told me about you?'

# CHAPTER THREE

'THE p-police?' Mallory swallowed, and stared out across the peaceful blue water. 'You've b-been to the police?'

'You are surprised?' The measured tones sharpened. 'You think I pull girls from the sea as often as fish?'

Silenced, she watched a dark-painted launch pass in the distance. For all she knew, it could be carrying some sort of marine police, just freed from the task of searching — she faced the idea with a shiver — for her body. He'd done exactly the right thing, she told herself miserably, and gathered courage to speak.

'Wh-why didn't you tell me straight away?'

'First, because you distracted me ——'

'I didn't!' she argued furiously. 'You needn't talk as if it were all my fault. . .'

'And then ——' he fixed her with stern eyes, daring her to interrupt again ' —— because we needed to eat.'

'As if that mattered!'

'It matters more than anything else,' he stated with tough, ingrained certainty. 'You western women get your food so easily, you have lost all respect for it.'

This at least she could deal with. 'I suppose you were brought up to value every crumb?'

'*We* were, yes. I and my four brothers. . .'

'Well, so was I.'

'You were?' He shot her a suspicious glance. 'But my family had to grow most of what we ate. It is not usually so with your people.'

44

'It depends which people you mean,' she retorted. '*My* parents had an allotment when I was little.'

'An allotment?' he repeated in disgust. 'Is this not a little piece of land you can tend or not, as you please?'

'We really cared about it!' She wouldn't let him put her down, she wouldn't! 'And my mother wasted nothing. She taught me to think of food as a——' Mallory paused to crush down a desolate memory of endless childhood hours spent alone at the table '—as a gift from the earth,' she finished in triumph. Who would have thought her mother's favourite tag would come in so useful? 'I was never allowed to get down,' she added, completely carried away, 'until I'd finished every scrap of my porridge, or my carrots, or whatever. . .'

'You *remember* this?' he asked, suddenly alert. 'Then by now you also remember your name?'

'No. . .'

She trailed off in dismay. The lie had seemed to drop from her tongue of its own accord, before she could think what she meant by it. What *did* she mean by it?

'It. . .it sort of comes back to me in bits,' she faltered. 'That bit came with a rush, because you made me angry.' She glanced timidly across to see how he was taking it. 'I. . .I sort of decided I wouldn't let you blame me for what another woman. . .'

She broke off, recalling the postcard she had inadvertently started reading, and tried another tack. 'Your wife was English or American, wasn't she?'

This time she meant to meet his eyes full on, but somehow couldn't. Instead she had to turn her head, and stare again at the dark launch whose wake was just reaching them in a long, V-shaped furrow. The curling lines of foam first lapped at their boat, then tossed it up and dropped it in a new rolling motion. Glancing once more at her companion, she noted with a catch of her breath how easily the lithe, soberly clad body rode the new swaying of the deck.

She dragged her unwilling mind back to her question. What had she been asking? Ah, yes, about his wife.

'Was she English, or American?'

'Neither.' He smiled, briefly and bitterly. 'But your guess is close.'

Not English, not American, but close? And English-speaking? Mallory wondered what such a nationality could be, then left it aside to pursue her argument.

'And she did waste food?'

'Often.'

'Well, I may not know much about myself——' she felt the blood beat at her temples with the deception '——but I know I don't do that. So please——' it came out more pleading than she meant, but she pressed on '——do stop being angry with me for what she did.'

He stared down at her, straight brows together over ember-dark eyes. 'This is not to the point, *devoika*.'

'It is! You said——'

'Enough!' His roar ricocheted from all the fibreglass walls. 'Be silent, woman, and listen to me.'

She huddled down, making herself as small as possible in the oversized shirt. After all, he was more right than he knew. She had, she could admit it to herself, been arguing to throw him off the track, been talking too much to hide the fact that she'd nearly given herself away.

And what for? What was she trying to do — stay here as a continuing burden on someone who had already done enough for her? She couldn't answer that even to herself. All she could do was to stare down at her rose-russet lap and wait, breathless, to hear whatever he had learnt ashore about her.

But he told her nothing. Instead he too stared at the

launch, until it rapidly became a rain-coloured speck in the sun-coloured sea-distance. Even then, when at last he spoke it was only to ask another question.

'So you still have no clear, useful memory? Nothing which would help us to return you where you belong?'

'I don't belong anywhere.' She could say that with chill certainty, because it was the simple truth. 'Not now.'

Simon and Linda Hawthorne had adopted her, she was sure, to try and save their marriage. It hadn't worked. They'd dragged on for a few years more, the allotment a last attempt to sink their differences in some common interest. They'd had a year's crops from it, and one hopeful spring, but already by the summer they'd been tending the young plants ever more grudgingly. The final, angry harvests had produced vegetables which Mallory, a miserable seven-year-old, hadn't wanted to touch. The following year, the plot had been left to the nettles and docks. The year after, Linda had moved to Norwich and taken her adopted daughter with her.

'I know I mentioned my parents, but I don't think they can be there much now,' Mallory went on with a caution she refused to try and understand. 'Or I wouldn't feel so alone, would I?'

Her companion did his confusing head-shake of agreement. 'You have already spoken of this loneliness.' He leant forwards, strong hands spread on denimed thighs as he considered the problem. 'But you must have had a reason for being here in Duni?' He looked at her beneath lowered brows, willing her to remember. 'You must have come on holiday? It is a holiday village. . .'

'I was alone,' she answered, not caring how sure she had sounded, because here too, after a fashion, she was telling the truth. 'Alone,' she repeated with a shiver, 'Like always.'

That loneliness, the great emptiness around and inside her, was something she had borne all her life. It was so much a part of her that she'd hardly noticed it until she'd met Richard and dared to hope it was over. Last night, when she'd found her hope betrayed and her dreams wasted, it had rushed in to reclaim her.

'Now I realise how foolish I was, but I know I didn't mean to get out of my depth yesterday.' She unclenched her hands, and spread them palm upwards on the rose-russet silk of her lap. 'And I. . . I know now,' she added with difficult honesty, 'how wrong I was not to thank you properly last night.'

She felt rather than saw the swift turn of his head as he studied her anew. Then he rose in a single smooth movement to sit next to her, his strong hands taking both of hers in a warm, steady grip.

'And you are glad now that I gave you back your life?'

She nodded, her hands motionless under the hardness of his. They really were unusually strong, and yet like the rest of him they flexed easily, as if much exercised in some special way. His nails were beautiful, each trimmed to a smooth oval which gave back the light as his fingers pressed hers.

'And now you believe me when I tell you that life here in Bulgaria can be a wonderful experience?'

She began another nod, then changed her mind. Timidly at first, then with an impudence she hadn't known she possessed, she raised her head and looked into his eyes.

'I should be saying yes like this, shouldn't I?' Hands still passive in his, she repeated the side-to-side yes she had learnt from him.

Close-up like this in the brilliant morning, she could

see why his eyes always made her think of fire. Like the rest of him they glowed with good health, the coal-dark centres shading out to an ash-grey which still shone almost black in contrast with the dazzlingly clear whites.

As she let her own eyes challenge the blaze of his, she heard the sharp hiss of his indrawn breath. Then his mouth relaxed to a fullness she knew and dreaded even while another part of her, the out-of-control part, fiercely welcomed it.

Slowly, with infinite reluctance, he dragged his glance from hers. 'You tempt me again, *devoika*.' His hands released hers to settle empty on his blue-denimed thighs.

'I. . . I know.' She couldn't pretend not to understand him. 'I think it comes on when I say "yes" your way. It makes me move my eyes like this.'

She tried it again, her hair bouncing on her temples and swinging down her back. Once more she found her eyes dancing their flirtatious message, though this time they spoke only to his splendid, forbidding profile.

Abruptly, almost convulsively, he stood up and took his former seat opposite her at a safe distance.

'You will have to bear yourself better than this, *devoika*.' He stayed turned away from her, distant and frosty. 'If every time you say yes, you make me wish to. . .' He broke off, stiffly upright on the bench. 'What will happen to us if you go on doing this?'

'To *us*?' Mallory blinked, wondering if she'd missed something. 'What could happen to *us*, except that you take me ashore and I. . .?'

She broke off. And I go back home, she'd nearly said, as if she knew exactly where that was and how to reach it. Which she did, only she had to pretend not to.

I wish I'd never started this, she thought in her confusion. I'll finish it right now.

But when she opened her mouth to speak, she couldn't. Where was home, anyway? Her mother's Norwich house, with the whole ground floor given over to the all-important medical practice? Her father's draggle-curtained flat in Bayswater, where their paths crossed once every three days? And for this she was to return to the hotel, and face Richard, and tell him why she'd walked away from him?

'What could happen to *us*,' she repeated weakly into the lengthening silence, 'except that you take me ashore, and I find out who I am?'

'Who you are. Perhaps we should think of this some more.' Still his glance stayed on the bright, inviting shore. 'You walked into the sea, you say?'

'Y-yes,' she admitted, hating herself all the more for letting him waste effort on a problem that didn't exist. 'In. . .in the dark.'

'In the dark, yes.' The fiery eyes stayed resolutely away from hers. 'But you wore clothes?'

'I. . . I don't know.'

She spoke the new lie with a sinking heart. Who could blame him for keeping his distance, after she'd behaved so badly? And this was worse, this entangling fabric of untruths, and she knew it, and she wasn't going to stop.

'A robe, maybe?' she added, making it sound like a question. 'A bathing-suit?'

'The people who clean the beach found a bathing-suit this morning.' He turned to her at last. 'In two parts, with padding here.'

He spread both hands ludicrously before his wide chest. Mallory glanced down in chagrin at her own inadequate breasts.

'You saw it?'

'Blue, it was, with white flowers.'

'I. . . I suppose that could have been mine.'

'They found it at the edge of the water.'

'And took it to the police?'

'You cannot remember wearing it?' Once more he had countered her question with one of his own. 'Or taking it off?'

She stayed silent, unable to answer except with another lie.

'You cannot remember how you come here to Duni?' he persisted. 'Or why? Or who with? These parents you spoke of? By now they must be crazy with worry for you——'

'If they were,' she interrupted bleakly, 'if I had parents who cared that much, would I feel so alone?'

She bowed her head against his penetrating stare, and felt, rather than saw, how he accepted the argument. When she dared to glance his way, she saw that the perfectly defined muscles of his arms had tensed, and he was leaning forwards over the long, tight-drawn lines of his blue-clad thighs as if he meant now to deal with something difficult.

'You who are made for love.' The ember-dark eyes swept up to hers, then swiftly down. 'Is it possible that you came here with a lover?'

'Wouldn't the same apply? Would I feel so alone, if I had a l. . .' She gagged on the word, unable to use it for the wretch who had lured her here. 'If I'd come here with a man?'

'You might have quarrelled.'

Mightn't they just! If she'd stayed with Richard last night, heaven knew what they'd have said to each other. As it was he could think what he liked, report her absence as he pleased. . .

Report her absence! But of course he'd have done that long since, with a description, and exact details of her name and circumstances, so that the police could set about looking for her. She stared in bewilderment at her companion.

'You must have found out all about me anyway.'

'You are sure you have left no grieving lover?'

Richard, grieving? She tried to picture it, then dismissed the idea to study the man opposite. Why was he asking all these questions? Why was he answering none of hers? Was he hiding something? And yet he'd seemed so forthright. . .

'Worrying parents, grieving lover — *you* tell *me*.' She scarcely noticed her own renewed evasions in her concern to understand his. 'Who is it who's been reported missing?'

Instead of answering he straightened, and looked beyond her in obvious relief. A vigorous masculine greeting sounded across the water, and while he answered it with equal vigour she turned in her seat to see that it came from an open white boat dipping up to them with two ruggedly handsome fishermen on board. It was the older man who had called the greeting, while the younger at the oars went on rowing.

'Are they friends of yours?' She noticed how the two had the same dark hair and eyes. 'Relations, maybe?'

'Just people who know me.'

He shouted something else across to the other boat. The younger man rested his oars to stare at Mallory with open admiration; the older made some teasing comment in which she thought she could distinguish a name. She repeated it under her breath, and it made perfect good sense. The brief exchange over, the oars dipped again and the other boat glided on out of range.

'They are from Sozopol, near here.' Her companion spoke fast and a little unevenly. 'That C before their number, that is an S in our language.'

'They're so like you.' She stared after the retreating

pair. 'What was that they called you? Was it——' she tried it aloud '—Nikolai Antonov?'

'It is my name.' Suddenly and for no visible reason much more at ease, he surveyed her with an odd air of expectancy. 'You know it?'

'I feel I should.' Once more she had that vision of women crowding round him in fluttering summer clothes, and once more she couldn't pin it down.

'No matter. I joked with them about the boats of Sozopol, which the fishermen there always call ships.'

'That wasn't the only thing you were joking about.' She was able to meet his eyes steadily at last. 'They were talking about me, weren't they?'

'It is nothing.' He settled his back against the bulkhead, and swung his feet up to the bench. 'A compliment, merely, on the new beautiful woman I have found.'

Mallory brushed aside the flattery as she always did. 'Do you bring lots of beautiful women out here, then?'

'Some. In Bulgaria we have many such.'

'I can believe it.' She glanced across the water at the two fishermen, small in the distance now but still moving with the same effortless grace she had noted in the figure opposite her. 'So the women here are as remarkable-looking as the men?'

'They can be very beautiful, yes.' He shrugged, following the progress of a distant windsurfer. 'As you are.'

'Oh, me. . .' She trailed off, intent on her own line of reasoning. 'You said they were "people who knew you". What a strange way to put it, as if——' she frowned, working it out '—as if you didn't know them.'

'Is that so strange?' he asked lazily. 'Many people know me.'

'You mean you're famous?'

'I would not call it famous.' He stretched on the bench, enjoying the sun. 'I have a name of sorts, if you are interested in the sport.'

'Sport?' She sat up to stare again at the strong-moulded profile. 'Wait a minute, I've got it.' She held up a hand to stop him speaking. 'Sport, sport, sport. . .'

Football? No, that didn't fit with this maddening elusive memory she was chasing, the memory in which a flock of summer-clad women gathered round a tall figure in white. . .

'Tennis!' she announced in triumph. 'You're Nikolai Antonov, the tennis star.'

'I was. I have moved on since then.' Dismissing the subject, he returned her gaze with sudden directness. 'You know my name, and yet you cannot remember your own?'

Mallory gulped. There she went again, showing how well she could remember things. Wasn't it high time she told the truth, that she knew perfectly well who she was, she just didn't want to *be* that person any more? But when she spurred herself to speak out, all she achieved was to close her eyes with an air of immense concentration.

'I can't remember it *yet* —— ' she managed to sound as if she were really trying ' — but it might help a lot, my having been able to recognise you. Can we talk about you some more?'

'If you must,' he answered, reluctant to give up his own probing. 'What do you know that would help?'

'Well, at Wimbledon you always played in the mixed doubles.'

'But I was never at my best on grass.'

'And the women — girls, I suppose — used to fuss like anything. Follow you in the street and things.'

'Such nonsense!'

'But you left tennis and went into business about——'
she put her hands over her closed eyes to concentrate
her banker's memory '—about four years ago. Market-
ing Megan Howell Designs in Germany, and America,
and Japan. . .' Her eyes flew open. 'So that's who your
wife was.'

'Was, and is not.' He underlined the last word with an
angry upward sweep of his head, a movement so quick
and decided that even his springy hair stirred from its
determined lines. 'She now has her rat-man.'

'Edward Burnett.' The name came to Mallory's
tongue unbidden. 'He took over the business from you.'

'He did not.' The dark eyes flashed. 'Megan did that
herself, so sure she could manage on her own. But
always he waited. . .' The expressive mouth snapped
shut, refusing to let out more.

Mallory frowned out to sea, not needing to act her
concentration this time. 'Surely Howell's is in trouble at
the moment?'

As a banker, she kept up with the financial news.
Megan Howell Designs had, she knew, been one of the
success stories of the last five years. The Welsh dress
designer had first attracted notice by her tennis clothes,
most of all by the outfits she had created for her well-
known husband. He had left the sport to become her
business manager, and with his help Howell's had taken
off into world-class fame, though only for a while. Its
present struggles were making headlines on the financial
pages.

'It is going down fast.' Nikolai Antonov showed none
of the vindictive relish one might have expected. 'Soon
Megan will not be able to pay her debts. She is not so
good at managing as she believed. . .' He broke off
once more, this time with a sigh. 'At least I got out at a
good time.'

'Took your share of the profits, you mean——'
Mallory couldn't resist the urge to talk shop '—while
there were some?'

'I have a fortune in hard currency,' he confirmed, not
boasting, but stating a fact which he took for granted. 'I
can live well, in the most beautiful country in the
world. . .'

'So why aren't you happier about it?'

As soon as it was out she bit her lip, feeling the
impudence of the question. She'd been far too quick to
put into words what his dissatisfied manner implied.

'You sounded as if you were counting your blessings,'
she explained, shamefaced. 'To try and convince yourself how lucky you are.'

'I am indeed lucky.' He rallied, and might have
seemed superbly relaxed but for the tension in the wide
shoulders, turned always away from her. 'I have everything I hoped for when I came back here to live. . .'

'Everything?' In spite of all her efforts to restrain it,
her voice rose in question. 'Don't you want your wife as
well? Aren't you still in love with her?'

If he had hotly denied it, she would have known she
had hit on the truth. But he didn't. Instead, he turned at
last towards her, dark eyes arrogantly certain of their
own power.

'If I had ever really loved her, do you think I would
ever have let her go?'

Mallory recalled the slender perfection of Megan
Howell. The dark, much photographed Welsh beauty
radiated a confidence and magnetism which came across
in the smudgiest of newsprint and made her a fitting
mate for the spectacularly handsome Nikolai Antonov.

They're both so different from me, they could be
from another planet, she thought, oppressed with a
sense of her own drabness.

'So it was over,' she persisted, not quite able to believe it, 'long before you split up?'

'Whatever we had,' he confirmed as if admitting to a failure, 'it went long ago. We were married for five years, but by the end we had become ——' his expressive mouth hardened with distaste ' — no more than a business partnership.'

'I think that's how it often is,' Mallory offered, aware of the sensitive ground she was treading, 'where money's involved. I used to read of couples like that ——'

'It is not good enough for me!' he interrupted, fierce head up, assertive nose jutting. 'I will have for my wife only a woman who is willing to *be* a wife. . .'

He stopped abruptly, and swung his feet down so that he could face her. The dark eyes surveyed her now like a surgical probe, their swift calculation reminding her how this man had carved an empire in the unforgiving world of high finance.

'You say you used to *read* about such couples?'

Clearly the fact had just clicked into place and set off a whole chain reaction of possibilities. How quick he was after all, Mallory reflected with a chill down her spine, quick and frighteningly tenacious. When he wasn't being distracted by his own problems, that razor mind must be a force to be reckoned with.

'In what kind of book did you read such things?' he demanded into her strained silence. 'And for what kind of reason?'

'I. . . I don't know,' she quavered, glad she was able to offer the absolute truth to that scalpel gaze. 'I. . . I used to read a lot, I think. . .all kinds of things. . .'

'Can you remember more of these things? Anything which will tell us ——' almost, he was mentally shaking her ' — of the person you used to be?'

'The person I used to be,' she repeated slowly,

playing for time. 'The person I used to be.' She couldn't disguise her longing. 'You speak as if I'd stopped being that person.'

'You can never stop being who you are.' He declared it like a creed. 'I learnt that myself, in my time away from home — but it is you we speak of, *devoika*. *Devoika!*' The deep voice roughened impatiently on the word. 'You must have *some* other name than this? Or must I go on calling you "girl" until. . .'

He stopped short. When Mallory glanced at him she saw only a quarter-profile, the edge of one high cheek-bone and the exactly proportioned line from there to the stubborn jaw. Just as he'd done earlier, he had turned away from her to stare at the shore.

Slowly, as if he knew he must, he met her eyes once more. 'Until I row you back over there, and say goodbye to you,' he finished, dark eyes veiled and opaque.

Mallory was astonished at the pain, so strong as to be almost physical, which shot through her at the words. Hadn't she always known that this time out of time, this holiday from real life must end very soon? That she must stop being the carefree sea-girl whose life began last night, and go back to being the starved creature nobody wanted?

Nobody but men like Richard, she amended to herself, and shuddered away from what those men wanted.

'When. . .?' She let her breath go, took another, and tried again. 'When are you going to do that?'

'Do what?' He straightened with a sigh, as if his mind had been miles away.

'Wh-what you said. . .'

She caught herself back, ashamed of her own cowardice. If she couldn't speak the words, how was she ever going to face the thing itself?

'T-take me ashore,' she amended, 'and s-say goodb. . .and send me back to wherever I came from. When,' she repeated, glad it was out,' are you going to do that?'

'When I have told you——' the dark eyes held hers '—what I must tell you.'

'So you did find out who I am.' She slumped in misery. 'Why didn't you say so before, instead of asking me all those things you didn't need to know?'

'I did need to know them.'

'But the police must have told you. . .'

'They told me nothing.'

'But. . .but how could they not?' She stared at him in genuine bewilderment. 'They must have been searching. . .'

She trailed to silence, suddenly reminded of her own puzzled questions which the passing fishermen had interrupted. And since then he'd tried yet again to help her remember what he believed she'd forgotten, as if he didn't know any more than she pretended she did.

'No one——' the dark eyes held hers with a new intensity '—has been reported missing.'

'What?'

She put her arms together and hugged herself over the rose-russet silk. How could there be no news of her disappearance? It had never been much, the tiny, insignificant life of Mallory Hawthorne, nobody would miss it, but now she felt as if it had never happened at all. She'd gone, and nobody was looking for her. Nobody cared enough even to find out what had become of her.

'You're. . .you're sure?' she stammered, still trying to take it in.

'As sure as I can be without. . .' But now it was his turn to hesitate. 'Yes,' he said as if he knew it wasn't enough. 'I am sure.'

'But the bathing-suit?'

'Was on display as lost property. Everyone is joking about it.' He paused. 'You can imagine such jokes for yourself.'

'That some woman decided to swim naked?' Hearing her own shaky voice, she realised she was trembling. 'That some couple made love at the edge of the water?'

'And that the woman forgot to dress before she returned to her room, *da*.' He absently gave the side-to-side nod which went with the yes in his own language. 'Such things are common enough in any holiday place, I suppose.'

So much for the hue and cry Mallory had imagined. She stared across at the peaceful shore, still trying to take in all the implications of what he had told her. Over there within those tiny peach-coloured arches, Richard was dealing with her disappearance in some way she'd never begun to consider. How on earth was he explaining it? And her robe; what had happened to her robe?

'So. . .what do I do now?' she asked, still winded by the news. 'I. . . I must have come from somewhere.'

'Another boat?' He glanced towards the open sea. 'Rich men sometimes bring their yachts this way, although——' he shrugged, admitting it was a long shot '——I saw none while I was fishing.'

'So I'm from nowhere,' she murmured numbly. 'I'm the woman from nowhere, who is nothing. . .'

'Calm yourself, *devoika*.' His voice was suddenly low and soothing, his whole powerful presence giving off an irresistible, wide-ranging reassurance. 'There is some answer to this, and we will find it.'

'We?' She turned to stare into the steady dark eyes. 'You'll help me?'

She saw at once that she'd mistaken his meaning. Worse, in her own need for someone to care about her, she'd asked too much of him. The long lashes had swept down like clouds over the sun, and he was shaking his head.

Wait a minute, though, this wasn't quite the head-shake she was expecting. This one, she realised with a surge of hope she did her best to suppress, meant *yes*.

'You will?' she whispered, not daring to believe it. 'You'll help me find out who I really am?'

And it won't be Mallory Hawthorne, her disturbed mind threw at her. Mallory Hawthorne's gone for good. The woman he'll help me to find will be someone quite different. . .

'I will help you, *devoika*.' His quiet voice cut in on her thoughts. 'But first, you must hear the rest of what I have to tell you.'

'There's more?' she asked, depressed.

'You speak as if more could only mean worse,' he commented, unusually hesitant. 'And so it is. . .'

'You're putting off saying it, aren't you?' she cut in, steeling herself. 'Well, don't. I can take it.'

'You do not understand, *devoika*.' The flashing gaze lowered before hers. 'It is for myself that I put it off.'

'But why? Where do you come into it?' She stared at him, bewildered anew. 'What've you done?'

'It is what I have not done.' He seized the opening she had given him. 'I have not told the police about you. I have not,' he rushed on, determined to finish now he had begun, 'told anyone at all that you are with me.'

# CHAPTER FOUR

'So I really don't exist.' Mallory shivered in the warmth of the strengthening sun. 'Not there ——' she nodded at the shore '—and not here. Nobody would ever know,' she added, aware for the first time of possible danger, 'if you threw me overboard.'

'Return you to the sea, after the trouble I had to take you from it?' Nikolai Antonov smiled at what was clearly, to him, an absurd idea. 'In daylight, in these waters you would soon be picked up, *morska devoika.* Perhaps by the fishermen who saw us together.'

'Oh. I'd forgotten them,' she admitted, curiously comforted. '*They* know I exist, don't they?'

'But still you are right to fear me,' he pointed out, serious once more. 'And yourself too, I think.'

'Yes.' She instinctively let her head droop, so that her hair swung forward and hid her burning cheeks.

Nevertheless, because he had spoken so simply of this other danger, she found she could be equally direct.

'Would you force me. . . Nikolai?' She brought out the unfamiliar name like a talisman.

His eyes acknowledged this, her first use of it. 'I would not need to. . .*devoika.*' The deep voice caressed the last word, his name for her. 'But still it would be wrong, to risk that you bear a fatherless child.'

'No. That wouldn't be right, would it?

A fatherless child. She swallowed down her chagrin at the cold, rejecting phrase. What had she expected— that he would promise to be a real father to any child she might conceive with him? Perhaps that he'd marry her, a nameless sea-waif he'd known less than a day? Both were out of the question, and she knew it, yet she had to ask.

'You'd. . .you'd leave your own child fatherless, Nikolai?'

'*No*!' The answer snapped out sharp and instinctive, the fire-smoke eyes blazing into hers. 'But I would rather he did not come from a moment of empty passion.'

A moment of empty passion. Mallory acknowledged the simple good sense even while she flinched from the hurt of it, but still the hurt was overwhelming.

To cover it, she picked on something far less important. 'Why did you say "he?" For all you know, it might be a girl.'

'He would be a boy,' Nikolai declared with absolute conviction. 'My family always has boys.'

Her heart lifted at the certainty of it. This was a man who knew, clearly and surely and right back through the generations, who he was and where he came from.

'Your family,' she murmured aloud for the pleasure of speaking the word. 'Didn't you say you had four brothers?'

'My parents have five sons, yes.' The fire-smoke eyes lit with a new expression, one of affectionate pride. 'My mother did her woman's duty, and more.'

'By having sons?' Mallory felt her hackles rising.

Confirming that he really meant the outrageous thing he'd just said, Nikolai Antonov did his side-to-side nod. 'Women are made for this.'

She winced as if he had just thrown cold water over her. What smugness! What simple, undisguised male chauvinism! Had she really been dreaming a moment ago of *marrying* this—caveman? Why, he was worse than her macho father!

'Women aren't. . .mere vessels to carry male seed,' she snapped, understanding her own mother's feminism better than she ever had before. 'They're people in their own right.'

'And my mother is certainly that,' he agreed, unabashed. 'You will see.'

'That's all very well, but. . .' Mallory broke off as his last words sank in. 'What d'you mean, I'll *see*?'

'I will take you to my family in Dragalevtsy,' he announced calmly, the decision settled. 'You have made me understand how it is the best thing to do with you.'

'I have?' She blinked, stunned by this whole new future he was opening to her. 'But. . .but you can't! What'll they say? What'll they think? What'll you tell them?'

'The truth, of course,' he answered, surprised she should ask. 'And they will believe it, and welcome you as a stranger who has lost her way.'

'But Nikolai, you can't just. . .pass me on like a parcel! I mean. . .' She shut her eyes tight and shook her head, trying to gather her wits. 'We haven't finished here yet, have we?'

'I think we have.'

The whole project was mad, and yet there was a perverse comfort in it. He meant to take charge of her, to give her a complete new identity. . .

In a family who believed that a woman's whole and only use in life was to bear sons? The idea spurred her to renewed protest.

'It would be a kind of. . .abduction! You talk of taking me to this place. . .what did you call it?'

'Draga-lev-tsy.' He drew the name out a syllable at a time, serenely superior to the ignorant foreigner who had never heard of it. 'It is a village near Sofia.'

'You want to take me there ——' she shook off his

condescending lesson in pronunciation '—when you haven't even made the proper enquiries about me here?'

'Of course I enquired,' he retorted, stung. 'Do I not wish to know all I can find out about you, *morska devoika*?'

'You've a strange way of showing it, not even going to the police. . .'

'That is another thing entirely. If there are *official* enquiries, you might leave. . .' He stopped as if he'd said more than he intended, then quickly continued in a new direction. 'I did visit each hotel in turn, and listen to all the gossip.'

'You did?' She strained forward, her mind racing in circles which were already becoming all too familiar. 'And you really found that none of them has anybody missing?'

'None.' He did his head-back, head-forward no. 'There was only one English couple here——'

'*Was*?' She felt the blood hammering in her ears. 'They've gone?'

'Very early this morning.' Clearly he had considered this pair himself and dismissed them. 'They heard of Rose Day at Kazanlük, and left early to fit it into their tour.'

'And those really were the only English people here?' she asked, puzzled. 'Did you find out their names?'

'One name only,' he corrected with distant disapproval. 'I know it is less and less the custom with your people, but these two were married.'

'Or pretending to be,' she retorted, thinking how Richard had insisted on their travelling as a married couple.

From the start, she'd disliked the deception. Arriving at the hotel, she'd squirmed to hear that her father had left a message for her under her assumed name. When

she'd returned the call, and he'd told her of that earlier
woman signed in to an earlier hotel under the same
name, it had seemed yet another sordid detail of a
sordid story. Detective Inspector Hawthorne had simply
and correctly deduced that he'd find her registered true
to pattern as Richard's wife.

Trying to forget her self-loathing, she asked again
about this other, unknown English couple. 'So what *is*
their name?'

'Something that reminded me of your English Robin
Hood. Nottingham?' Nikolai frowned, his disturbingly
handsome head on one side while his straight black
brows drew together in thought. 'But no, that was the
sheriff, was it not?'

Mallory could have made her own guess, but didn't
dare. She could only try to conceal her inner trembling,
and wait while he raised an outspread hand, commanding the memory.

'Sherwood!' He snapped his fingers in satisfaction.
'That is who they were — a Mr and Mrs Sherwood.'

Mr and Mrs Sherwood. Mallory bit back the urge to
shout it aloud, and tried to set her agitated thoughts in
order. What on earth was Richard up to now?

'You're sure he — this Mr Sherwood — was. . .'

She choked to silence. She had only just stopped
herself asking if he hadn't been, after all, a man
suddenly and mysteriously alone.

'You're sure you didn't see them?' she finished
lamely.

'I have already told you no, *devoika*,' Nikolai replied,
tolerant of her slowness. 'The desk clerk thought Mrs
Sherwood very beautiful in her English way. . .'

'She seemed specially English, then?'

'Both were very reserved and correct.' He briefly
mimed his own Bulgarian version of the ramrod correct-

ness of the traditional English couple. 'Besides, they
have left to continue their holiday in the Valley of
Roses. There can be no connection.'

'I s-suppose not,' she agreed, even while her heart
thumped at the new lie. 'N-none at all.'

'Very well.' He rose in a businesslike manner. 'We
will go to Dragalevtsy, and my mother will look after
you there until you are more yourself.'

'Here, wait a minute. . .'

But already he had flicked a switch just within the
cabin. An engine boomed to life somewhere below, and
thumped over in neutral while he sprang to the deck
above the bench where he had been sitting. Light-
footed in spite of his size, every move flowing with
athletic grace, he made his way to the nose of the boat
and set about raising the anchor. When the massive
double hook appeared above the water, he lifted it on
board as if it weighed nothing, deftly secured it to the
deck, and returned to the cockpit as smoothly as he had
left.

'Now look here,' Mallory began, scrambling out of
his way, 'you can't just —— '

'Quiet, *devoika*.' He seated himself at the tiller and
scanned forwards over the water, judging his course. 'I
am new with this boat; it needs all of my mind.'

Thus commanded, she could only obey. After all, she
realised forlornly, she couldn't stay forever in this place
apart, this holiday from life. Whether or not she went
where Nikolai said he would take her, she had to go
ashore some time.

But. . .to what? Certainly not back to Richard, even
if he hadn't already taken off somewhere else. She
fiddled with her hair, pulling it forwards to hide the new
flush in her cheeks, and wondered how he had managed
to make it seem as if she were still with him.

'You really don't know anything more about this English couple?' she shouted above the roar of the engine. 'For instance, why have they gone to this place with the roses?'

'Everyone goes to the Valley of Roses.' His deep tones unfairly easy to hear, Nikolai kept his eyes on the channel ahead. 'Especially now, in June. Even poor Mrs Sherwood, who had toothache in the night. . .'

'Toothache?' Mallory tried to fit this new piece into the puzzle. 'And still they left?'

'It was better by then.'

'But. . .but wouldn't the driving make it worse?' she floundered, glad of the engine noise to blur her confusion. 'Wouldn't there be pot-holes and things. . .?'

'Certainly not.' Nikolai dragged his mind from his navigation to give her an indignant sideways glance. 'Our Bulgarian roads are as good as roads anywhere.'

Silenced, she added this new item to the rest, and reviewed them in order. Toothache. English reserve. The planned sightseeing tour brought forward two days, on the trumped-up excuse of this Rose Day, whatever that was, in the place whose name she had already forgotten.

'Kazanlük,' Nikolai obligingly repeated when she asked him. 'I would take you to this Rose Day, *devoika*, but it is not until the end of the week.'

Yet Richard had already departed for it. Mallory could almost feel the facts whirring in her brain, adding themselves up.

He's run away, she decided. He gave out that I had toothache to explain why I wasn't about, and now he's got the hell out.

'Did anyone see. . . I mean,' she amended, 'how did Mrs Sherwood seem this morning when she left?'

'Again I tell you, *devoika*, I did not see her.'

And nor had anyone else. Mallory knew it as surely as if she'd heard it from the hotel staff herself. She was just opening her mouth to speak again when Nikolai pointed with an imperious gesture to the cabin.

'I cannot have these questions at this time,' he announced, his cool authority unmistakable even over the engine's heavy vibrations. 'Go and wait below.'

'Just like that?' She flung her head up in astonished anger. 'Of all the overbearing, bossy. . .'

She paused. She'd been perfectly determined not to move, but, after all, she did need time to think. The more private her thinking the better, and it might be quieter below. With all the dignity she could muster in her fluttering rose-russet draperies, she stood up on the vibrating deck.

'I'm going because I want to, not because you told me to.'

'Go, *devoika*.' He wasn't even looking at her, just taking it for granted she'd obey.

And she did, without another word.

The engine noise was if anything louder in the cabin, but it worried her less now that she was alone. She seated herself on one of the berths, and gave her new suspicions full rein.

The more she considered it, the more likely it seemed that Richard had behaved as though she were still with him. Having explained her non-appearance with this story of toothache, he'd somehow pretended she was in the hired car while he'd dealt with the luggage and settled the bill. Then he'd been free to drive off to some new place where nobody knew she existed.

And why had he acted out this elaborate charade?

Why, Mallory deduced with bitter logic, to avoid the scandal.

He must have guessed what her father had told her,

and what she'd done, and his only reaction had been to get away before the enquiries could start with their inevitable publicity.

And so far he's made it, she surmised, repelled by the cold, selfish deviousness of the man she had believed she loved. He'll have taken my luggage with him. That only leaves a bathing-suit that could be anybody's, and a robe. . .

But no, he wouldn't have left her robe behind. She knew now why the cleaners hadn't come across it on the beach this morning. He must have brought it in himself last night. Already by then he must have started making his plans.

The cowardly bastard, she thought with renewed fury. He didn't care what had happened to me, only that it shouldn't come out while he was there to be involved in it.

Presumably now, as soon as he judged it safe, he would travel as a single man. He'd return any way he could to his everyday life, and when news of her disappearance came out he'd deny ever having known her.

Not that my father'll let him, Mallory thought, comforted by the memory of Inspector Hawthorne's determined, vengeful pursuit of any suspect. He'll nail the. . .the double-dirty *scum*.

Her father's word leapt unbidden into her mind, and with it a new sense of shame. After all, Richard wasn't a criminal. He couldn't be accused of anything but having made a fool of her and run away from the consequences.

Which is just what I did myself, she realised, hating her own cowardice. I walked out like a wimp, instead of showing Richard up for the worm he is. . .

'Wake up, *devoika*!'

'What?' She came to herself with a start to find

Nikolai standing over her, stooping a little as he had to in the limited space of the cabin. 'What is it?'

'We have arrived. Do you not see?'

'Oh! N-no I didn't.'

She gazed wonderingly out of the wide-open cabin. Here was the white-arched hotel close-up, and a café bright with umbrellas, and carefree holiday-makers coming and going in the brilliant sunlight. He had brought the boat into a marina and secured it by the stern so they could easily step ashore from the cockpit. Through the long portholes she could see other boats moored in the same way.

'I didn't even notice you tying up,' she admitted, feeling foolish.

His heart-melting smile shone forgivingly. 'You were dreaming.'

'Nighmaring,' she murmured under her breath, and tried to give her mind to current problems. 'What now?'

'We go ashore, of course.'

He took her hand to draw her to her feet. Languorous pleasure coursed through her from the contact, but she resisted, staying where she was despite his gentle, insistent pulling.

'I can't go about like this.' She indicated the copious rose-russet garment which was her only covering, and lifted her foot for him to see. 'I haven't even got shoes.'

'You should never wear them.' He kept her hand in his, but suddenly, smoothly, he had lowered himself to sit with her. 'Such perfection ——' he stared at her still-extended foot ' — should not be covered.'

'Er. . .' She dropped it quickly. 'That's all very well. . .'

'Did you know that your feet curve and skim like sea-birds?'

'Like wh-what?' She turned to him, mindlessly transfixed by the hundred arrows of heat which stole into her from his nearness. 'Nobody's ever said anything like that to me before.'

'That is because there is so much else to say of you.'

'There is?' She shot a hunted glance at the sunny quayside, and hastily avoided the interested stares of the couple strolling by. 'Er—look. . .'

'Your eyes, for instance. You have the eyes of a wild stag.'

'A *stag*?' she echoed, struggling to break the spell he was casting over her. 'A stag's a *he*.'

'You wish me to say, of a doe?' He made a small, amused sound deep in his throat. 'But it is not so. The doe's eyes are soft and melting. Yours are not.'

'They certainly aren't,' she retorted with another glance to the quayside. 'Not here. . .'

'Not anywhere. Always your eyes are wild and secret, like the stag's. And your skin is all ivory.' His finger stroked down her cheek, leaving an unbearable hot longing in its wake. 'Last night the ivory was sea-cooled; this morning it is sun-warmed. Then there is this——' he touched the corner of her mouth '—like an opening rose.'

She opened it in good earnest to say something off-putting, but all that came out was a wordless gasp. He had brought his fingertips to her lower lip, caressing it until it yielded to the burning pleasure of his touch and prepared itself for she knew not what.

But *I* do know what, she thought with a last swooning effort. He's going to kiss me, right here, almost in public.

She tried once more to stiffen away from him. His hand cupped her chin, and turned her face gently up to his, but she could easily have shaken free of that. It was his eyes which held her, those ember-dark eyes with their underglow of heat which spoke without words to a part of her quite beyond her control.

And that part signalled its own response. She recognised it despairingly, a wordless message for that same wild, secret self he had so clearly described a moment ago.

Several times already this morning, this other Mallory had threatened to take charge of her. Each time Nikolai had helped her to keep it in check — so why was he encouraging it now? She tried a last pleading question.

'Why are you doing this, Nikolai?' The words stumbled from her reluctant tongue over heavy, yearning lips. 'It's the wrong time, and the wrong place. . .'

'It is exactly the right time,' he responded, his own lips as full and ardent as hers. 'Exactly the right place.'

'But everybody who comes by can see us.'

'So I can speak at last without danger.' He didn't say what danger, but his tone did. 'Ever since I found you I have watched your feet, your eyes, your mouth. . .'

'You didn't talk like this when we were out at sea.'

'I wanted to. And what would have happened then, *devoika*?'

'I. . . I don't know. . .'

'You do.' To prove it, his lips possessed hers.

And just as she had always known she would, she accepted them. She could do no other. She had been seeking all her life for this gentle fusion which turned so quickly to a new hunger and a new exploring. She only needed to reach her hand up so, and press the stiff hair so, to feel it spring up again as she knew it would. Her fingertips of their own accord sought the hollow at the nape of his neck, and strayed from there to the steely muscles of those girder shoulders, and lingered for the delight of feeling their living strength under the knitted cotton. . .

'Oh, please!' she gasped when he took his mouth from hers and thrust her hand gently from his body. 'I must touch you.'

'And I you,' he murmured, still husky but with an undertone of iron good sense. 'But this kind of must, we must not.'

'So why did you start it?' she demanded, desire souring as awareness came rushing back. 'You didn't have to.'

'I did. I had to speak to you, *devoika*.'

'You didn't!' she protested, angrily avoiding the gaze of the two teenagers who were ambling by. 'Not here. . .'

'Here. These words have been boiling in me ever since I first saw you, and now they are spoken.'

'Spoken and got rid of. Good on you!' she retorted, ever more furious that he should choose to torment her like this. 'So what'll you get rid of next — your inhibitions? Your clothes? Your. . .your seed that always makes boys —— ?' She stopped as his hand clamped over her mouth like a velvet-covered vice.

'I do not like to hear such talk from a woman, *devoika*.'

'*You* don't. . . Of all the. . .' It was no use, she couldn't form the words or get them out beyond his muffling hand.

Nor could she shake him off. She tried jerking her head back, but still his hand stayed in place over her mouth. She had to be content with what her eyes could shoot at him, those wild eyes he'd talked about which now felt wild enough for murder.

'As you say, I have now got rid of the things I had to tell you.' His voice still held a husky trace of passion, but mostly it was filled with the satisfaction of a mission accomplished. 'I will not need to speak so again.'

'Big deal!' she tried to say, but only blew a shapeless sound against his palm.

'You tickle, *devoika*!' Releasing her at last, he leaned superbly sideways from his seat next to her, courteous as if they had just met in a drawing-room. 'I think you wish to say something?'

'Don't I just!' she rapped back at him. 'If you do anything like that to me again, I'll scream the place down.'

Unimpressed, he smiled his heart-melting, condescending smile. 'Then you must learn not to speak so freely, *devoika*.'

'And what about the way *you* spoke?' she demanded, beside herself with rage. 'What about you. . .paying me all those compliments. . .?'

'No compliments,' he contradicted, mildly indignant as if she'd accused him of some kind of social double-talk. 'Everything I said was true.'

She refused to be deflected. 'You said all that stuff after I'd asked you not to. After I'd reminded you——' she scowled out at the small boy who had stopped to admire the boat '—that we were in public. In *public*,' she repeated as he gave the child a fatherly grin and a word of greeting in his own language. 'Will you listen to me. . .?'

'I heard, *devoika*. But if we had not been in public, I could not have spoken at all.' He watched the boy skip away, and turned to her with his usual air of practical common sense. 'I can never say such things to you while we are alone.'

'You can't?' She blinked at the upside-down logic. 'Why not?'

'Only think,' he urged, the soul of reason and good conduct. 'If we had been private just now, we would have made love.'

'Oh, you. . .'

She clenched her fists, but couldn't argue. It was, after all, the truth, however little she liked being reminded of it.

'So I spoke publicly, where we cannot do what we both wished to do,' he finished with ruthless exactness.

So that was what he'd meant about the time and the place being right. It was, she had to admit, a point of view.

'The only other possibility was for me not to speak at all,' he added, and shot her an enquiring glance. 'Would you have liked that better?'

She could only sit in silence, recalling the things he'd said. And to say them in such a way, he must have really meant them. . .

'N-no.' She couldn't meet his eyes. 'No, I. . .' Unable to go on, she raised the foot he had likened to a sea-bird, and stared blindly down at it until she heard his sighing exclamation.

'You are right, though. We must find you shoes, and clothes that fit.' But he didn't move, or make any sign of wanting to begin the task.

Nor did she. 'Where will we get them?'

'There is a shopping mall here.' Still he lingered at her side. 'The right thing now would be for me to take you to see this lost-property bathing-suit.'

She nodded, not needing to have it explained. She had been naked in the sea; a bathing-suit had been washed ashore. The conclusion was obvious.

'Almost certainly it would help for you to see it,' he added with a hesitation totally unlike his usual decisive style. 'You might easily remember how you. . .how you lost it, and why.'

Mallory took a deep breath, and plunged once more into the lie she had created. 'Y-you think it might be mine, then?'

'It is your size.' His sideways glance flicked over her belted rose-russet slenderness. 'But I do not like to think of you wearing such a thing.'

'It's quite decent. . .' She floundered to a halt, fearful that her hasty reply had given her away. 'Isn't it?'

'Decent enough. But I do not want you to be the kind of woman who would wear. . .' As before when he'd described the bathing-suit, he sketched a padded front to his rangy chest.

'Why not?' She glanced down at her small breasts under the rose-russet silk. 'I don't see the harm.'

'Maybe not, but your body is already perfect.'

He offered a strong, flexible hand in commanding invitation. Without her will her own stole out to it, her mind refusing to acknowledge what it was doing until she felt her palm nestled to the warmth of his.

'Also, you should never, ever——' the ember-dark eyes held hers, intense yet unreadable '—ever pretend to be anything but what you are.'

In the silence that followed she had the feeling of a pact being formed, even of vows being exchanged. When she spoke again it was with the almost ritual calm which seemed the only right response to what was happening between them at this moment.

'And what am I, Nikolai?'

'This,' he told her, weighing each word, 'is what we are going to find out.'

'You think we can?'

'We can, *devoika*. We can.'

In some way she didn't understand, the question of the bathing-suit had been settled. They weren't going to see it or consider it further.

'And now——' all his usual certainty returned as he rose and drew her upright with him '—we go ashore.'

And ashore they went, up three concrete steps and

across a pavement to a low, expensive car with darkened windows. Nikolai opened the passenger door and she folded herself with relief into the leather-scented seat. Only while she waited there alone, watching Nikolai give the boat into the keeping of a uniformed attendant, did she think to ask herself what she was hiding from.

After all, she told herself, nobody's gone missing. Mrs Sherwood's in the Valley of the Roses, whatever that is. I'm not her, and nobody's looking for me.

Feeling more free to be herself than she ever had in her life before, she relaxed behind the tinted glass. A bronzed couple glanced in at her as they strolled by, and she returned their open, casual stares with one equally casual, equally open. The only identity she had left was as the woman who'd just come ashore with Nikolai Antonov. Nobody knew any more than that about her, not even herself.

'Where now?' she asked when he had settled in the driver's seat. 'I'm still not dressed to go among people, am I?'

'You think not?' He surveyed her sideways. 'Many go barefoot at the seaside.'

'And this shirt?'

'On you, it could be for the beach.'

'It could?' She raised her arms to look down at herself. 'I wish I could see!'

'However,' he admitted with a brief smile, 'the beach is one thing; Dragalevtsy is another.'

'Exactly,' she agreed with enthusiasm. 'Hey, wait though ——' as she realised how she had gone along with his cool assumption '— that doesn't mean I'm going to Draga-whatsit with you.'

'You had better learn to say it, *devoika*. Seatbelt.'

'What?' She saw that he was already wearing his. 'But we haven't. . . I told you I'm not. . . Here,' she exclaimed in alarm as the car glided along the quayside, 'where are you taking me?'

'You will see.'

'Not to Draga. . . Draga. . .'

'Lev-t-sy. Say it, and put on your seatbelt.'

'All right then — Dragalevtsy!' She angrily buckled herself in, reluctantly obedient on both counts. 'You needn't think I'm going there with you. . .'

'I told you, Dragalevtsy is near Sofia. A long way.' Already he had guided the car out of the hotel complex, and into the pine forest. 'I will show you.'

'You will not,' she contradicted, a little panicky. 'You can't take me all that way without even asking me first!'

'I will show you on a *map*.' He emphasised the word with good-natured patience. 'Do you not have maps in England?'

'So where is it, this map?' She opened the empty glove pouch, and turned to survey the empty back seat. 'It isn't here.'

'You will see it.'

'But *where*? If you aren't the most maddening——'

'And when you have seen it,' he went on with his usual air of sound good sense, 'then you will know exactly where we are going.'

Mallory gritted her teeth. 'So I don't get to be asked.'

He shrugged. 'I will ask you if you wish.'

'Taking completely for granted that I'll say yes.'

'Of course you will say yes.' He didn't even bother to look at her, just changed gear and kept his attention on the narrow road. 'What else is there for you to say?'

What else indeed? She felt a new chill as she realised again how she had put herself into his hands. Officially, she no longer existed. He could do what he liked with her. How on earth had she got into this?

But she knew how. She only had to glance sideways at

that star-defying profile to feel a new surge of that optimism and confidence which the mere sight of him always inspired in her. She couldn't explain it, didn't even want to. She only knew that somewhere within her, deeper than thought could reach, deeper than logic, deeper than worldly experience, somewhere deep as the beating of her heart, she trusted him.

## CHAPTER FIVE

'VILLA Lamia!' Somewhere a long way off, Nikolai's deep tones had roughened in disgust. 'Is this not a foolish name?'

'Hmm? What?' Mallory blinked awake. 'Where are we? Have we come far?'

'A kilometre, maybe two.' He wasn't after all a long way off, but here in the car at her side, and for her as gentle as ever. 'I must let you rest, *lyubima*, before we travel on.'

She undid her safety-belt and stretched, the new word *lyubima* echoing round her head. 'What was that you just called me?'

'Nothing. You slept so peacefully.'

'And there's this name, Lamia, that you don't like.'

'It is nothing. We have work to do.'

But he didn't stir from the driver's seat. Mallory stared through the windows, wondering where he had brought her and why. Ahead, the narrow strip of smooth cobbles finished in a turning circle which suggested a private drive. All she could see from here were the pine trees which grew down the gentle slopes to the sea, and, on the up side of the hill, a wall of cream-gold stone.

'Weren't you talking about a villa?' she asked. 'This place with the name you don't like?'

'I was, and this is it.' He indicated the wall with a contemptuous movement of his head. 'She chose that it should imitate the Sozopol style.'

'She?' Mallory had seen this scorn before, and knew
who roused it. 'You're talking of Megan, aren't you?'

And thank heaven he doesn't speak of *me* like that.

The thought gathered cloud-dark in her sleepy mind,
and woke her as if the cloud had turned to cold rain. So
far this man had never shown her anything but kindness
and respect. Even the fire of his passion had been in its
own way tempered to the lost, disorientated creature he
believed her to be. He'd been a good friend, but when
she heard his anger she shivered to think how she was
deceiving him. He would make a terrible enemy.

'So what's wrong with the name Lamia?' she asked to
take her mind off this new fear.

'She wanted a dragon name, for Wales,' he explained,
ferocious as a dragon himself. 'She could have had Villa
Drakon, but no, only this other Bulgarian word would
do.'

'I expect she wanted that because it's also a girl's
name,' Mallory guessed timidly. 'Is it so very wrong?'

'A lamia is a serpent-woman who eats children.
Perhaps it fits after all,' he added with a mirthless laugh.
'Always she had her shows, her designs, her busy
life. . .' He put aside these thoughts, which clearly still
caused him pain, and turned the fire-smoke eyes full on
Mallory. 'Can there be people in your country who
would call their daughter Lamia?'

'They might if they didn't know what it meant,' she
murmured, still taken up with this unexpected glimpse
into his past. 'My parents didn't know what mine
means. . .'

She broke off, horrified. One unguarded answer, one
moment of caring more about him than her own shabby
secret, and she had given herself away completely.

'You have remembered your name? Your parents?'
Sure enough, he pounced on the clue. 'You said some-

thing strange about this last night, and I thought you were wandering. But perhaps you were not?'

'Wh-what did I say?' she stalled, playing for time.

'That your name meant evil, or unlucky. Think, *devoika*!' He took her shoulders lightly yet impatiently in his two hands, only just managing not to shake her. 'What can it be, the word that has this strange meaning?'

Pretending to be thinking hard as he had ordered, she closed her eyes to escape that all-seeing, ember-dark gaze. But it was only a temporary relief. Presently she had to face him again, and shake her head.

'I'm sure it'll come soon.'

She hoped it might be enough for him, but she should have known better. The strong hands cupped her shoulders, willing her memory to deliver the missing facts.

'You spoke of your parents. Can you not remember more?' The dark eyes burnt into hers. 'Try, *devoika*!'

'I'm trying.' Hating the lie, she hurried on to a half-truth she could utter with more confidence. 'I know it'll all come back to me soon.'

It had better. The shaming pretence had lasted long enough; she must find a way to end it. She couldn't go on like this, always in fear of the final betraying slip which would bring upon her that same contempt she had seen him show for his ex-wife. She shuddered, knowing clearly and surely that he would never forgive deceit of any sort.

'Things do come back like that, don't they, when you're not really looking for them?' she babbled much too fast. 'It happens when you're sort of. . .letting your mind rest. . .'

She gave up, unable to meet those deep, dark eyes any longer. Her own gaze dropped to her lap, where all her fingers had crossed against the lies she was telling. Please, please let him leave her alone now!

As if he would. 'A name that means evil, or unlucky.' Still he worked on it. 'There cannot be many like this.'

She must stop him. And suddenly, from some deep well of female understanding she had never suspected within herself, she knew how.

It was easy. His hands were still on her shoulders; she only had to lean towards him like this, turn up her face like this. . .

When his lips claimed hers, it immediately seemed like his idea and his alone. She could only accept him, rejoice in him, take fire from him and forget everything but his nearness and the forbidden rapture of his hands on her body.

'You shouldn't,' she gasped against his mouth. 'You said you wouldn't. . .'

'Did I?' He played with her silk-covered breast, circling and tantalising. 'And shall I stop?'

'Not there!'

'Here, then?' he took the peak that thrust its mute demand through the fine rose-russet covering. 'Is this where I stop?'

'No,' she pleaded. 'Please, Nikolai, not there!'

She didn't know herself what she meant. Washed by the piercing sweetness of his touch, frustrated by the different layers of clothing that held them apart, she could only yield once more to the timeless, mind-destroying pleasure of his mouth on hers. His hands took their way with her breasts, teasing them to new heights of demand and stirring ever deeper, ever more dangerous whirlpools within her until she tensed and loosened in turn, unable to tell pleasure from pain.

Somehow her improvised belt had gone, leaving the shirt to hang loosely about her. Then he had opened even that, and her yearning breasts were defenceless to his hungry gaze. His lips swooped to one coral crest and took it for his eager tongue to taste, and it felt so right, so wrong, the pleasure-pain so exquisite that she had to give voice to it.

'Please, Nikolai, oh, please. . .'

She broke off in mindless dismay. Whatever she'd meant by that light-headed cry, whatever she'd hoped for, it wasn't this. She'd never wanted his mouth to leave her breast, his hands to drag the loose shirt roughly back to her shoulders, his nearness to become farness as he put her away from him. When she dared look at him he had gone from her, withdrawn through the aching, endless distance to his own side of the car.

'Oh, d-dear,' she stammered, trying to make sense. 'What h-happened?'

'We made love,' he told her, still husky with banked-down passion. 'As I swore we would not.'

'Is th-this too private a place to be safe, then?' she gasped, hastily settling the shirt and refastening it.

'It is a bad place for what we were doing.' But he was beginning to regain his composure. 'Old Stefan or his wife might come out at any moment.'

'And wh-who are they?' Mallory groped for the hooked elastic belt, her face burning at the idea of these respectable-sounding strangers finding her as she had been a moment ago.

Clearly Nikolai didn't like it either. 'They are friends of my family, and also Megan's caretakers,' he informed her tersely. 'Let us do what we must here, and be on our way.'

'And what exactly is this thing we must do?' She almost welcomed the return of her earlier exasperation. 'You still haven't told me.'

'We are going to make you ready for travelling.

Come!' He sprang from the car and walked round it with his usual loose-limbed grace to open her door.

'Hang on a minute!' She stayed where she was, casting about her on the seat. 'I haven't found my damned belt yet!'

'It is on the carpet by your feet,' he told her distantly, and let her reach down for it without his help.

Not that she minded. She was glad enough to pick it up, and to make a business of hooking it round her. Anything to put off the moment when she had to get out and face him. She had just remembered that it was she who had provoked this episode, seeking his kisses on purpose to lead him away from the question of the memory she had never lost.

What kind of person am I turning into? she wondered, hating herself. First a liar, now a teasing slut. . .

She swivelled in her seat with unnecessary force, and swung her feet to the cobbles. Her bare soles welcomed the uneven surface, hard and cool as the reality which might help her shake off this new, dislikeable self.

But even as she rose from the car and faced Nikolai in the pine-scented drive, she knew it wasn't that easy. The other self was still with her, tilting her head to look up at him, letting her dark hair brush his arm, making her eyes long and coquettish in their sideways gaze.

'You still haven't asked me,' she reminded him, 'if I'm willing to travel with you.'

Had she really intended that as a rebuke? It had come out soft and lilting as the bird noises among the rustling pine-branches. She saw his glance slide from her face to her dishevelled hair, down to the belted rose-russet shirt, and quickly away.

'We will discuss this when you are dressed, *devoika*.'

'And what shall I wear, Nikolai?' her other self crooned, tempting as Eve.

'We will see,' he snapped, and left her.

The coldness was like a blow in the face. She didn't know which was harder to bear, his abrupt rejection or the knowledge that she had done everything to deserve it. Or rather, she excused herself, the other Mallory had.

She trailed after him along the cream-gold wall. This had turned out to be a little higher than he was and capped with the same peach-gold tiles she had seen on the hotels nearer the beach. A dragon-shaped plaque of smart green copper announced the name of the house twice, once in Latin letters and once in what she took to be Bulgarian. The gold-brown door where Nikolai halted had its own tiled porch, and a doorbell guarded by another green copper dragon.

His ember-dark eyes swept over her as she joined him at the door. She answered their wordless enquiry with a penitent gaze, pushing her hair back into some appearance of order.

'Don't I look a bit oddly dressed to be paying a call?'

'Only as if you had just come from the beach,' he responded, unsmiling, as he pressed the bell. 'It is so near to Duni that they will be used to holiday-makers.'

'You haven't any keys?' she asked, still testing to find out if he'd forgiven her.

She couldn't tell from his absent reply whether he had or not. He no longer seemed to be thinking of her at all.

'I never lived here,' he explained, and added with a return of that frightening contempt, 'Megan did not either.'

'So why did she have it built?' Mallory pressed, somehow needing to remind him that she was here, and that she wasn't Megan.

'Another of her wasteful whims. As if she could ever have spent whole winters here,' he exclaimed, still irritated by that past time, 'so far from the nothing-people and nothing-events she really valued. Perhaps soon,' he added on a new thought, 'I will make her furnish it for real people to have holidays in.'

'You can do that?' Mallory stared doubtfully up at the elegant door. 'Even though you aren't married any more?'

'I can make Megan do anything I want, if it is worth my trouble.'

Mallory nodded. She could easily believe it.

'And this house is in Bulgaria, so it is worth my trouble. . .'

He broke off as the door was opened by a tall old man. With that snow-white hair he had to be old, Mallory decided, though his handsome features were more weathered than lined, and in that rough shirt and heavy trousers his bearing was as vigorous and upright as Nikolai's own. The two fell on each other with cries of greeting and joyful bear-hugs, then began a series of exchanges which sounded like questions and answers, cordial yet measured, each flowing courteously on from the last.

Mallory found herself listening carefully. This, she realised, was the first time she had really heard Nikolai speaking his own language.

And I like it, she decided. It's so straight and clear; I'm sure I could learn it. . .

She saw that the older man was offering his hand to her, and took it with equal politeness. Nikolai hadn't introduced them in English, but this must be Old Stefan — somehow she had to think of him as 'Old', as if that were his title. He was murmuring cordial-sounding phrases of greeting, so Nikolai must have explained her presence here, heaven knew how.

'What have you said about me?' she asked as they were led up a wooden flight of outdoor steps.

'Only that you may take some of the clothes wasting in the wardrobe these two years. . .'

'What?' She halted in the cool stone well of the steps. 'You're not expecting me to wear your ex-wife's clothes?'

'Of course not! This is stock she brought here to sell. Move, *devoika*,' he urged impatiently. 'You hold us both up.'

She saw that Old Stefan was already at the top of the steps, holding open a half-gate. She hurried up through it, and found herself in a vine-hung, dream-peaceful paradise.

'What a gorgeous terrace!' Enchanted, she snuffed up the scents of honey and pepper, and the freshness of leaves with the sun on them. 'And look, you can see the sea over the pines. . .'

'Of course you can,' Nikolai interrupted impatiently. 'Megan told the architect to plan it so.'

'Did she arrange this terrace?'

'She arranged nothing. Everything here —' he glanced up at the trellis with its shady, overhanging vines, and around at the flourishing plants in their blue pots ' — is the work of Stefan and Elena. *Haïde!*'

With the new noise of command he hurried her across the green quiet to another door. Old Stefan had already vanished through it, calling out some warning to whoever was within. By the time they entered the wide, cool, wood- and spice-scented room, a sturdy old woman was bustling across it.

'*Ya, Nikolai!*' Delighted, she dropped the copious white apron she had just removed from her ample waist, and folded him to her print-covered bosom.

While he answered her new and much faster flood of

questions, Mallory stared eagerly around. Hadn't he talked of this house being in the Sozopol style? Was that why the room had these white walls rich with carved wood panelling, the wood ceiling and floor, the wide window open to the summer scents of terrace and hillside, the bewildering number of doors? It must have been hard-working Stefan and Elena who had made a home of it, scattering bright rugs, hanging up the kaleidoscope-patterned plates, and installing the heavy, carved table and matching chairs which were the only furniture. And what was this intriguing earthenware vase in the corner, its pot-belly and narrow neck further connected by a handle with a hole. . .?

'It is called a *stomna*.' Nikolai must have noticed the direction of her stare. 'They keep it here for coolness.'

'Coolness?' Mallory wondered if she'd ever understand this strange world she had strayed into. 'For a *vase*?'

Perhaps the word was the same in Bulgarian. At any rate, Elena understood, and flung her head back in full-throated, good-natured mirth. Still laughing, she hurried to pick up the vase and raise it high. When a sparkling stream of water sprang from the hole in its handle, she neatly caught it in her mouth. Then she smilingly offered it to Nikolai, and he crossed the room to drink from it in the same manner.

'You need never touch it with your lips,' he explained as he returned the water-pitcher to its owner. 'Very practical.'

'I begin to think you're a practical lot, you Bulgarians,' Mallory murmured, approaching to accept the offered pitcher and drink in her turn.

She might have known it wouldn't be as easy as it looked. Water slopped over her chin, ran down her neck, and soaked her high, embroidered collar.

'No matter, we are done with this shirt,' Nikolai told her as Elena smilingly rescued the *stomna*. 'Make your greetings, and then we will go and find you more suitable clothes.'

'Make my. . .oh.'

She accepted Elena's offered hand as she had accepted Old Stefan's. She couldn't help but be cheered by the other woman's open, heart-warming smile and felt her own features relax in a way she would never have believed possible. Smiling herself, she watched Elena cross to pick up her apron, refasten it, and bustle away on her flat-heeled lace-up shoes.

'What nice people,' she observed as soon as they were alone.

Nikolai shrugged. 'They are Shoppe, like me. Shoppe vices, Shoppe virtues ——'

'Hang on, you've lost me again.' She held up a hand, glad that the new word was at least an easy one to say. 'Who are these Shoppe?'

'We are the people of the country regions round Sofia,' he explained, tolerant once more of her foreign ignorance. 'My father and Old Stefan looked after the sheep together when they were boys ——'

'He was Old Stefan even then?' she interrupted, amused at the thought of a shepherd-boy with such a title.

'There were many Stefans in his family,' Nikolai responded with dignity. 'And now, *devoika*, to business.'

'You were talking about Shoppe vices just now,' she grumbled as he hurried her towards one of the many inner doors. 'Would bossiness by any chance be one of them?'

'One of our *virtues*,' he corrected her in a mock-reproof, 'is to get on with things. *Haïde*!' He opened the door and gestured her through it.

Still Mallory lingered. The room she was about to see must surely, more than any other in the house, belong specially to Megan Howell. She found herself strangely reluctant to enter it. Instead, she carefully shaped the commanding word he had just thrown at her for the second time.

'Hhh-a-ee-day,' she pronounced sound by sound. 'Why have you begun saying that, Nikolai?'

'I suppose it comes naturally when I speak Bulgarian,' he told her impatiently. 'It means come along, get going, move—anything you want it to mean. Or as now——' he reached past her and pushed open the door '—stop wasting time.'

Thus commanded, Mallory hesitantly entered the room. Inside she had to pause again at once, overwhelmed by its endless, empty, rose-patterned, glittering space. Only the open window relieved the sense of emptiness. Helped by the green and blue reality of pines and distant sea, she could sort out the rose pattern as carpet and the dazzling infinities as mirrored walls and ceiling, endlessly reflecting each other.

Only they weren't walls after all, but cupboards. Every one of the four sides had a cupboard with mirrored double doors, and those cupboards were its only furniture. The whole room was nothing but a great big wardrobe.

She shot one glance at the nearest image of herself, an endlessly repeated rose-russet intruder with the watchful darkness of Nikolai at her shoulder, and turned hurriedly back to him. 'So it's only a dressing-room after all.'

'It was planned as our bedroom if I had allowed it,' he growled in disgust. 'Can you imagine making love among all these mirrors?'

Mallory could, and disliked the idea as much as he did. 'You'd never be able to get away from yourself.'

'Exactly. But then,' he added, explosively bitter, 'some people are more fascinated by themselves than by anything else in the world. . .' He broke off as if he had said too much, and made one of his sweeping gestures round the room. 'The cupboards are not locked. Choose what you will.'

'All right.' She approached her own slight, wide-eyed figure in the nearest double doors, and saw endless copies of it, back and front, down corridors of distance. 'I hate all these repeating images of myself. . .'

'Then we do this.'

He walked briskly round the room and flung open each set of doors in turn. When he had finished, all the mirrors faced into each other, reflecting nothing but themselves, and the room had become a series of cedar-lined cabinets brilliant with garments of every imaginable colour.

'Goodness.' Mallory took down a strapped mini-dress of slashed mandarin-red. 'Would Bulgarian women really buy this?'

'Who knows?' He surveyed the garish thing with dislike. 'But she meant to organise a boutique down in the shopping mall, for tourists.'

'I do see people might wear this sort of stuff on holiday, to show off a tan.' She touched a blue-green skirt, discovered it was mostly fringe, and let it drip away through her fingers. 'So why didn't she start her boutique after all?'

'Megan never had any follow-through.' He didn't return Mallory's smile at his tennis-player's phrase. 'She started everything, finished nothing.'

'It's easy to see why Howell's is going down fast without you.' She stared at a cupboard filled with shoes on racks, another of silk underwear, another whose shelves were crammed with sunhats, hair ornaments, perfume, cosmetics, and hung with stylish bags of all sizes. 'All this stock doing nothing but go out of date ——'

'Enough, *devoika*!' Nikolai walked abruptly to the window as if to refresh himself with the blessed reality of pine-trees and sea. 'You had better hurry, or Elena will have the food ready before you are dressed to come to the table.'

'She's cooking for *us*?' Mallory looked up in surprise from the rack of sandals. 'I didn't know we'd be eating here.'

'Do you think they would let us leave without?'

'*Nice* people,' she murmured, suddenly carefree. 'I do *like* Bulgarians, Nikolai.'

He half turned from the window, straight brows lifted in gentle irony. 'You know others besides these two?'

'I know *you*. . .'

She stopped in dismay, and instinctively turned away from him to hide in a rack of skirts. Had he understood her, she wondered, as she had suddenly understood herself? She clashed the hangers along their rail, snuffed up the scent of roses and cinnamon that pervaded this particular cupboard, and told herself that it just couldn't be so. She couldn't possibly have fallen in love with someone she hadn't yet known for a full day.

'I have shown you the clothes, *devoika*.' The deep voice from the direction of the window sounded a little husky, a little uneven, but otherwise much as usual. 'Now you will do better without me.'

'Y-yes.' She didn't dare look round at him, but heard his light, firm footsteps, muffled by the thick pile of the carpet, crossing the room to the door. 'I'll. . . I'll see you when I've finished here, then.'

He closed the door, and left her free to rush to the window where he had been a moment ago. Breathing the clean scents of the pines, resting her eyes on the unchanging line of the sea, she heard again in her mind the last thing he had said to her.

'Now you will do better without me.'

As if I ever would, she thought on a sudden wave of anguish. In just half a day you've made me need you, Nikolai Antonov, as these trees need the sun!

She knew now why she had pretended to forget everything about her past life. From the moment she'd met him it had all ceased to matter. None of it had any significance, except as the track she had needed to take through the world to find him.

And now I've found him I won't lose him, she told herself. I can't! I'll follow him barefoot. . .

Which was exactly what she had been doing. The thought sent her hastening back to select simple beige sandals in the smallest size available. They fitted, and she kicked them off only long enough to scramble into silk briefs and a divided skirt of crocus-patterned cotton. Then she replaced the rose-russet shirt with one in plain crocus-yellow cotton, and tucked it in with a sigh of relief. She was respectable at last. . .

Wait, though. As she began to close the mirrored doors, her tousled reflection returned to remind her that she hadn't finished until she'd tidied her hair. She found an ornamental comb from the hat cupboard to straighten its tangles, and a crocus-yellow band to hold it off her face, then paused to stare at the shelf of cosmetics.

She wanted to look her best for Nikolai, didn't she? She had no time for make-up now, but she could take some with her. This beige airline-style bag would hold it and another outfit to change into, and then, seeing it had so much space left over, what about adding a really nice dress?

The one she chose was of some knitted material that didn't crease, in a dramatic black-purple that reminded her of ripe plums. She found lipstick and nail varnish to match, and a shimmery eyeshadow a little lighter, and sparkly high-heeled sandals the same colour. Everything went easily into the main compartment of the organiser-bag, and now all she had to do was hang away the rose-russet shirt. . .

But when she picked it up she found she couldn't bear to leave it. Breathing in its scent of roses and cinnamon, she felt as if she were trying to discard a part of herself, and worse, a part of Nikolai. She couldn't let it go, not when it was so easy to fold and drop into the bag. She zipped it out of sight, and now at last was ready to return to her only love and go with him anywhere he would take her.

He was waiting for her at the carved table, a motoring-map spread before him. 'You look nice, *devoika*,' he commented, straightening to look her over. 'I did not know that Megan had brought any such womanly clothes here.'

'Womanly?' She glanced down at the shirt and divided skirt.

He shrugged. 'Modest, if you will. Sensible. Pretty, but not too bold.'

She considered this list of the qualities he felt a woman should have. 'Are your Shoppe women like that?'

'The best women everywhere are like that.'

'I bet Megan Howell isn't.'

'Forget Megan.' And he laughed, softly but wholeheartedly, as if he had suddenly begun to enjoy himself.

'But for you I would never have come to this house, but because you made me ——'

'Wait a minute,' Mallory cut in, carried away by his high spirits and the answering delight they had roused in her, 'it was *you* who made *me* come here.'

'You needed clothes, did you not? And the clothes are here, are they not?' He held up that commanding hand, refusing to let her argue. 'So it was *you* who made *me* come here. And I thank you for it, *morska devoika*.' His glance swept once more over her tied-back hair, and the practical, pretty outfit she had chosen. 'I see now that you have cleansed this place for me.'

'Oh,' she breathed, thrilled. 'Have I really?'

'Be careful.' The ember-dark eyes blazed at her under the straight brows. 'If you go on looking at me like that, I will have to come to you and kiss you again.'

'And. . .' She swallowed, unable to take her gaze from his, unable to conquer the hopes and fears that chased around her mind '. . .would that be so bad, Nikolai?'

'For now, yes,' he announced with his usual certainty, and beckoned her to the table. 'Come, I will show you where we are going. Here is Sofia.' He indicated the Bulgarian capital on the spread-out road-map. 'Here is our Mount Vitosha, and here, though they have not space to mark it, is Dragalevtsy.' His index finger lingered at a point between mountain and city. 'You see how well we are placed? We have peace, good air, a ski-lift ——'

'I see it's a long way,' Mallory interrupted, surveying the network of roads from coast to capital. 'Almost the other end of the country.'

'An easy day's journey,' he assured her. 'Bulgaria is not so very big, not in kilometres.'

'Only in everything else?' She finished the idea for him, and they laughed together.

'But it is true; we are a great nation,' he asserted with patriotic pride. 'For five hundred years we suffered and stayed unbroken, a nation still. It was here at Shipka——' he pointed to the map '—that we cast off the Turkish Yoke. I will show you the place of the battle.'

'Oh, how I'd *love* that!' She bent over the map, alight with his own enthusiasm, and saw that Shipka was a little off the direct route. 'Have we time?'

'We have time for everything now, *devoika*. All the time in the world.'

'But won't it stretch out that easy day's journey to—to Dragalevtsy?' She raised her head, proud that she could now pronounce the name of his home village. 'Not that I mind. . .'

'So why should it not be a *week's* journey?' he demanded. 'I would even say a month, but that would be greedy. A week, though. . .' He let the delightful idea hang in the air between them.

And indeed, why not? Mallory recalled, with a new sense of shock at how everything had changed for her since then, that her holiday had only begun yesterday. For a whole week, nobody would even miss her. For a whole week she could be free as she had never been before, alive as she had never been before. . .

'I have so much to show you, *devoika*!' Intent once more on the map, he had already taken her consent for granted. 'Our Horseman of Madara, our old capital at Türnovo, our beautiful Stara Planina mountains. . .' He went back to the map, intent on finding ever more riches to lay before her.

'You really have time for all that?' she murmured, unable to believe her luck.

'I have time for everything. *We* have time for everything,' he corrected himself. And for the end of this week,' he finished in triumph, 'like this Mr and Mrs Nottingham I told you of, we will go to Kazanlük for the Rose Day.'

'Do you mean——' Mallory felt suddenly cold '—Mr and Mrs Sherwood?'

'You remember their name better than I do.' The ember-dark eyes narrowed. 'Yet you cannot remember your own.' He wasn't asking, simply stating a fact for storing away in that busy, organised brain. 'Is it not a strange thing, this memory of yours?'

The bright dream quivered between them, fragile as a soap bubble. Any minute it might break, and leave nothing of all its swirling colours but a drop of cold water. She couldn't let that happen, she couldn't! She drew a deep, calming breath, and with it realised that all she needed to do was tell the simple truth.

'I can remember everything you've ever said to me, Nikolai. Every little thing.'

'And I you, *devoika*.' His arm at her waist turned her to face him. 'And I you——'

They sprang apart as a mellow, feminine voice cut through their timeless solitude. Elena had come to fetch them for the midday meal, and so, following her across the room and through another of its many doors, they held safe their soap-bubble dream for a little while longer.

Perhaps I can keep it for a whole week, Mallory thought. Perhaps even for longer.

They needn't go to this Rose Day. Or if they did, if she couldn't prevent it, then most likely Richard wouldn't be there. Most likely he'd have managed to get himself home long before then.

And if he hadn't? If she went to this town of roses and came face to face with him?

I'll worry about that when I come to it, Mallory told herself, and all the colours of the dream danced round her as she entered the cool, tiled kitchen.

# CHAPTER SIX

'So MUCH not seen, so much not done!' Nikolai regret-
fully folded the map, and accepted a menu from the
white-clad waiter. 'But we knew before we started that
a week would not be long enough.'

Mallory could only sigh, and go on drinking in the
sight of him across their outdoor table. Between the
red, traditionally embroidered cloth and their blue and
red umbrella, the midday sunlight hung rosy and dif-
fused. Its shaded glow added extra colour to his ivory-
gold, copper-gold, teak-gold tan, and stirred fiery
sparks in the smoky eyes which met hers enquiringly.

'You are thoughtful, *devoika*?'

'Hmm? Oh.' She roused herself. 'I was only watching
the way the light clings to you, as if. . .'

She stopped. As if it loved you as much as I do, she'd
almost said. Luckily she'd caught herself back in time.

But she couldn't stop looking at him. As usual he
wore no tie, and the collar of his long-sleeved white shirt
was open over the vitality of his tanned throat. She had
come to realise that his dark grey trousers and casually
open, matching waistcoat, though severely plain, were
his own everyday version of the brilliantly sashed and
embroidered costumes of his people. He was asserting
by his dress that he was Bulgarian, and she loved him
for it.

But then, what didn't she love him for? She sighed
again, and flicked a petal of withered blossom from the
crocus-blue shirt she was alternating with the crocus-
yellow. She would have to come to terms with the

frightening fact that their week in paradise was nearly over.

'Of course a week wasn't long enough,' she answered his earlier comment at last. 'Eternity wouldn't have been——'

'Enough of that!' He clashed the plastic-covered pages of the menu together and regarded her over them, the sparks catching fire in his smoke-dark eyes. 'You are no more ready for eternity now than when I took you from the sea a week ago.'

'*Nearly* a week ago,' she corrected him, jealous for every fragment of time left to them. 'We still have two days.'

'Perhaps we will have more, perhaps not. Whatever happens——' the fiery eyes compelled hers ' — you must never again try to take eternity for yourself, *devoika*. Promise me that.'

'I don't need to. Really not, Nikolai——'

'Promise me!'

'All right.' She let herself be drawn to that deep, dark, fiery gaze. 'I promise.'

The moment hung between them as had so many during this last glorious week. Always the questions had been held back, the comments unspoken, the past and future put away in some other dimension, to be dealt with later.

There had to be a later, they both knew that. They'd known it for five days, ever since he'd stopped the car somewhere on the winding coast road beyond the Villa Lamia and told her that she couldn't go on without a travel document of some kind.

'No hotel will accept you without one.'

He'd spoken without looking at her, and just then she hadn't wanted to look at him either. Ahead through the windscreen she could see little flaws of wind coming and going on the blue of the water, and a quiet beach of silver-gold sand edged with silver-white, ruffling waves. This place was beautiful enough for any dream, and yet already the real world was perilously near.

'And. . .and how do I get one?' she asked, thinking of her own perfectly valid, legal passport which must be somewhere in Richard Sherwood's luggage.

'There might be a British consul in Burgas or Varna. If not, we will have to apply in Sofia. . .'

'And give a name,' Mallory finished, suddenly cold in the mellow sunlight of late afternoon.

For a long time he didn't answer. Then, still not looking at her, he undid his safety-belt and leant forwards to pull something from a back pocket. He passed it to her, and she stared down at the battered document.

'A passport?'

She opened it on a photo of a dark, vividly pretty face, small-featured and large-eyed as her own. When she read the name she frowned, and when she saw that it was valid for some years yet she nearly dropped it.

'How on earth can you still have this? How did she get out of the country without it?'

'How indeed?' he growled in remembered exasperation. 'The fuss we had in Sofia when she found she had lost it!'

'So that's how you know about going to the consul?'

'Every traveller should know that. Though Megan,' he added scathingly, 'did not.'

'So the British consul in Sofia gave her a temporary travel document,' Mallory guessed, beginning to understand. 'Which got her to England, where——' she turned a sideways, enquiring glance to his austere profile ' — she sorted it out and got a new one?'

'Where *I* sorted it out for her and got her a new one.'

'But it's made out to Megan *Howell*,' Mallory had been calculating from the date on the passport, 'though it must have been issued during your marriage. . .'

She trailed off. She herself had come here as a supposedly married woman, but with an official name quite different from that of her supposed husband. Richard had dismissed her objections with the comment that many women these days refused to change their names on marriage.

'Megan was a very independent woman,' Nikolai confirmed with a sarcastic edge, an echo of that earlier bitterness, in his deep voice. 'Or so she liked to believe.'

'Oh, my goodness!' Mallory exclaimed, appalled by her sudden, vivid sense of how he must have felt, this proud Antonov, to have his name so rejected. 'Why on earth did you marry her, Nikolai?'

'I thought I was in love with her.' Now at last he faced Mallory, the ember-dark eyes unveiled in passionate confession of past weakness. 'Against all sense, against all reason, against all experience, I wanted her as my wife.'

Mallory returned that passionate gaze until she couldn't bear it any longer. Then she glanced down again at the passport, and reflected that Megan Howell must have been mad not to accept this marvellous man, name and all, forever. Forever and ever, from this day forward. . .

She dragged her mind away from such fantasy, and back to the reality of one surname or another. 'It only meant she kept her father's name, instead of taking her. . .her husband's.'

'This I told her. But it was also her professional name,' he added in a quieter tone as if he, too, was turning his mind to more practical matters. 'So I let her have her way.'

Yes, it would have to be like that, Mallory realised with a pang. He was a man who knew what he wanted and how to get it, but he would always listen to his wife's views, and consider them, if he loved her. And he would have to love her. He would settle for nothing less.

'So where *was* this passport, after all?' She tried to keep the envy from her voice. 'I suppose you found it later, after she'd got another?'

'Long after the divorce,' he confirmed, 'on the only visit I ever made to the Villa Lamia before today.' Exasperation returned to the deep tones. 'It was on the floor, propping up the short leg of her drawing-table.'

'Oh, my goodness!' Mallory exclaimed again. 'Was she really that scatter-brained?'

'Scatter-brained. I like this word.' His tension eased on a small note of enjoyment. 'Yes, Megan was most scatter-brained.' The enjoyment fading, he stared ahead once more, reliving past anguish. 'I should have returned it to be cancelled, but somehow. . .' He left the idea unfinished, his reluctance speaking for itself. 'I put it in her desk, and forgot it until now.'

'When you thought we might use it.'

Mallory weighed the open passport in both hands. At this moment she felt very much Inspector Hawthorne's daughter. She could almost sense her father looking over her shoulder, silently horrified at what she was thinking of doing and trying to tell her what it would mean.

'Travelling on someone else's documents ——' she had to say it ' —is a criminal act, Nikolai.'

'I know.'

And here it was again, the soap-bubble dream about to be crushed by implacable, factual reality.

'So,' she began heavily, 'we spend our time trying to find a consul here at the coast. . .'

'Or we go to Sofia at once. It will mean driving through the night, but that is not so bad.' He turned to her, scrupulously refusing to put any pressure on her to reject the clear, sensible, law-abiding course. 'You will like Sofia——'

'Can I think about it for a minute?' she interrupted quickly. She felt, rather than saw, his side-to-side movement of the head to mean yes. Her mind was busy with that photograph of a face enough like her own, that name of a woman who had once been his wife. . .'

'I suppose,' she ventured at last, heart thumping, 'it would mean our always booking a double room?'

'No.' This time he nodded his vigorous negative. 'In Bulgaria also, a wife gives up her father's name and takes instead the name of her husband.'

'So everyone would expect your wife to be Antonov, like you.' Almost without noticing, she did the side-to-side nod she had been practising. 'But still. . .surely Megan Howell was known as your wife?' She glanced down again at the passport. 'Apart from which, she's well known in her own right.'

'Not in Bulgaria.' His emphatic response made it clear that his ex-wife's prized name meant nothing here. 'I am sometimes recognised, but Miss Megan Howell need only be an English friend travelling with me.'

An English friend called Megan Howell. Why, Mallory realised with a sense of shock, the initials are the same as mine.

Somehow, that settled it. The wild, unreasoning part of her took over so quickly that she hardly recognised it was happening. All she knew was that she had snapped the passport shut, and unzipped the special pocket of the flight-bag from the Villa Lamia. Even the very pocket seemed to fit with what she was doing, designed as it was to hide away this usurped identity until she needed it for her own illegal purposes. Her decision made, her criminal career begun, she zipped the passport out of sight.

'So at last I've got a name, Nikolai,' she announced to his unreadable, star-defying profile, 'of sorts. For a week.'

'One week.' He turned slowly to face her. 'It is not much to ask for.'

'And when it's over?' The question was out before she could stop it, thrown out by that other, wild part of her whose needs and desires were so impossible to restrain.

Weren't they? She quailed at the shrewd, questioning light in the ember-dark eyes so near her own. Perhaps she had better teach restraint to that other Mallory, or risk losing even this one week.

'When it is over ——' his quiet response confirmed her fears ' — I think you will somehow remember your own name.'

She found she was staring at her hands, suddenly clenched together on her crocus-bright lap. The other part of her, the wild Mallory, wanted to meet that shrewd dark gaze and give up, admit at once that she'd been pretending.

She even found herself preparing to ask when he'd guessed. But if she did that their soap-bubble dream would vanish forever. And its loss, she knew instinctively, would hurt him as much as herself. She didn't know why he was going along with her pretence, but she did know that if she wanted to keep him with her, if she wanted this week which meant so much to both of them, then her wildness must be recognised, accepted as part of her, and mastered. And so she fought it, and won, and stayed silent.

'But for now, for one week ——' perhaps he understood the struggle within her '—I am your guide to this most beautiful land. For one week——' the deep voice caressed her like the gentle, remembered touch of his hands '—you are nothing to the world, nothing to anyone but me. Nothing but my *morska devoika*.'

'Your sea-girl,' she murmured, and dared once more to look at him. 'Will you teach me Bulgarian, Nikolai?'

'Anything, *devoika*. If I can teach it and you can learn it, that is,' he added more cautiously. 'Within these limits, I will teach you anything you wish to know.'

'Anything?' On a wave of longing, she passed the tip of her tongue over her lips. 'Really anything?'

She could feel it like a physical force, the power that drew her to him. It kept her gaze hopelessly entangled with his, made her fingers ache to comb that springy hair, made her mouth heavy with the need to meet the passion in his. . .

'All but this.'

The exclamation, in a voice both hot and cold together, sounded as if it had been dragged out of him. Hot for her, cold for himself, he forced the blade of his safety-belt between them and grated it shut, letting it cut them off from each other like a sword on a pillow.

'There will be no more of. . .of what we both wish——' for a moment desire was almost too much for him, but he quelled it with tightened lips '—until we both know what we are doing.'

And with that he restarted the car, and kept intact their fragile dream. Rejected, trembling, ashamed, she knew he was right. It would have been so easy to grab the pleasure of the moment, to taste and treasure and become one, easy as eating a new and dangerous fruit. But they just didn't know what to expect from each other. Until they learnt, until each could give again the trust that had once been betrayed, she could only honour him for his restraint, and learn from it.

And learn she did. They dawdled along the coast, careful and courteous and apart, always apart. She went each night to her separate room, and left it each morning strengthened by sleep and ready for all the new pleasures he was teaching her. They had nothing to do with sex, these pleasures, but there was friendship in them, and harmony, and a growing awareness of Nikolai as a person and not just as a gorgeous male creature.

'That's crazy,' she protested when he told her his family nickname of *malko*, and the reason for it. 'You, the little one?'

They were taking an evening stroll through Varna at the time, and she had to crane sideways to look up at him. At this promenade hour the cosmopolitan streets were crowded, but none of the men they passed was taller or more handsome than Nikolai. Yet here he was telling her that he'd been, in effect, the runt of the Antonov litter.

'I am the youngest,' he pointed out. 'And, though I am now thirty, I am still the smallest. And the. . .how do you say it?' He sought for the word, and found it. 'The plainest.'

'That——' she craned sideways again, loving the bold, heroic, infinitely satisfying lines of him '—I simply cannot believe.'

'Ah, but you have not seen my four brothers.' Family pride shone from the ember-dark eyes. 'In Sofia, heads turn when Vassil walks down the street. And Traiko's wife will not let him from her sight.'

'So that's why you never got conceited about your looks.'

'I do not understand you, *devoika*.' And the direct gaze down into hers showed that he meant it. 'Even if I considered such things, what would I have to be conceited about?'

'Oh, Nikolai, I do. . .*like* you!'

And I do, she told herself now for the umpteenth time while she opened her menu. He's a wonderful man. He isn't just handsome, and strong, and clever; he's *good*. . .

'I think you are dreaming again, *devoika*.' His voice reached her from beyond the shiny pages of the menu she was supposed to be studying. 'If you tell me you are busy choosing what to eat, I will not believe you.'

'Well, I've already chosen, so there.' To prove it she closed the menu, and named the dish which was her favourite because it came from his own part of Bulgaria. 'I'm having Shopska salad.'

'And for this you searched so long?' he teased. 'You always have Shopska salad.'

'And *shishkebab*,' she supplemented, unashamed.

'At least leave the *shishkebab* for today. You will have plenty of those tomorrow, at the Rose Day.'

'Oh. Er—yes. I will, won't I?' Suddenly she wasn't hungry any more. 'Maybe I'll just have the *tarator*, after all.'

'Only that?' He surveyed her with straight brows raised. 'This cold soup is good, but it is not much.'

'It'll be enough. Really. It's a hot day. . .' To prove it she fanned herself, though the air was cool enough under their bright umbrella.

'As you wish.' He gave their order, and reopened the map to spread between them. 'So the question is, which way shall we go to Kazanlük?'

That wasn't the question at all as far as Mallory was concerned. If she had only dared to say so, she didn't want to go anywhere near Kazanlük, or any other part of the Valley of Roses.

'Why can't we stay in Veliko Türnovo instead?' she asked, making out with difficulty, upside-down, the name of the ancient capital. 'You said it's spectacular. . .'

'Veliko Türnovo is there all the year round,' he stated unanswerably. 'The roses are not.'

She was silenced. They'd had this discussion already, and many more. She'd been fascinated to learn of this exotic crop, harvested every year for the distilling and exporting of precious, incomparable rose-oil. Perfumes all over the world depended on Bulgarian roses, but the roses could be picked only when they began to open, and they opened when they chose.

So the timing of the Rose Days was never known for long in advance. It was only by luck that there was to be one during this week, and how could she turn away such luck? Especially when it meant refusing something so rare, so poetic, so much in keeping with their dream as a festival to celebrate the gathering-in of a harvest of roses.

Yet how could she go to it when their one week, precious as rose-oil itself, might be ruined forever by it? When it might bring her face to face with Richard Sherwood, and everything she had rejected on that night when she'd walked into the sea?

But it's a long time since he left Duni, she comforted herself. He might be anywhere by now, even back in England without me. . .

'*Tarator, kavarma*.'

The waiter set their dishes before them, and wished Mallory good appetite in slow, lilting English. And, after all, the *tarator* proved as delicious as ever, its yoghurt with chopped cucumbers and walnuts another of the many small pleasures she had learnt to enjoy here in Bulgaria with Nikolai.

'You will know, of course,' he observed, daring her not to know such an important fact, 'that yoghurt was invented by the Bulgarians?'

She hadn't, but was happy as ever to learn from him. 'That explains why it's so good here.'

'Some people think it is the secret of why Bulgarians live to such great ages.'

'I think you're just a healthy lot.' She emptied her plate, and sat back for the other pleasure of watching him finish his casserole. 'You don't in the least need all those spa treatments you hand out at places like Pomorie.'

'If you have them, use them.' He laughed briefly with her, but sobered at once, as if his joke had reminded him of something uncomfortable.

'You're thinking of your own gifts,' she guessed with that quickness between them they had both come to accept as normal. 'And that you should be using them.'

'I have been lucky.' He put his knife and fork together, and signalled to the waiter. 'But luck should be shared, not wasted.'

'I like that way of looking at it,' she agreed, absently nodding from side to side in the Bulgarian way she was starting to take for granted.

The waiter removed their plates. Nikolai, not needing to ask what she wanted, ordered coffee.

'I was born with a talent to play tennis, and given the training to develop it,' he began when they were alone once more. 'Then with my marriage I found I also had some talent to organise, to administer. . .'

'To make money?'

'The money may have been only the luck we are speaking of,' he amended, modest and hard-headed as ever. 'But now I have it, I must use it right.'

'And what's your idea of using it right?' She realised

she sounded a little condescending, the banker giving advice, but was too intent to care. 'I hope you've already got it safely tied up, and earning good percentages?'

He gave her a withering glance. 'I do not need this first lesson in finance, *devoika*.'

'Sorry!' But still she couldn't suppress her own hard-won banking skills. 'So what have you in mind for it?'

'First, to bring in more foreign currency.' This time he responded comfortably to her professional interest. 'Equal first, to give me a useful job in life.'

'Another business empire?' she suggested. 'You could do it. You made Howell's the international success it used to be ——'

'*Ne!*'

His chin shot up, square and stubborn. The Bulgarian word for no, already sharp and clear, was further underlined by his emphatic nod.

'I spend no more time in offices among businessmen.'

'So let's sort out how you *do* want to spend both your money and your time,' she answered with the briskness which came so easily to her in her everyday banker's life. 'For a start, where do you want to live? No, wait, I needn't have asked that.'

The banker in her abruptly gave way to the woman. Before she could stop herself, she had met the dark eyes with a smile so unguarded that all her love must surely be in it for him to see. She caught it back, almost felt herself pull it in and button it down, before she went on in something as near as she could produce to her clipped banker's tone.

'The only place you'll consider living now is here, in Bulgaria. Right?'

He did his side-to-side yes, his eyes releasing hers to

their chosen professional distance. 'In Dragalevtsy, if I can.'

But it wasn't so easy to stay professional. Already she had lost the coolness she was struggling for, wistfully unguarded as she tried to imagine being so attached to one place.

'It's really as good as that?'

'It is home,' he answered cautiously, and then responded from the heart. 'But yes, it is very good. You will see.'

'Will I, Nikolai?' She felt a new sigh escape her. 'I do hope so.'

'So do I, *devoika*.' As usual he had understood her at once. 'So do I.'

And here it was again, that unknown future which was now so near. Mallory could feel its myriad possibilities humming about her like a locust swarm, eating up their precious dream day by day, hour by hour, minute by minute. . .

But still there was coffee. The waiter set the copper tray on the table between them, and she summoned her hard-learnt Bulgarian thank you.

'*Blagodaria*.' As always, she couldn't help smiling at the strange, explosive noise the word made in her mouth.

'*Molya*,' the waiter replied, taking the word for granted but giving her an answering smile as he departed.

She checked over the tray for the pure pleasure of looking at it. This particular cone-shaped copper jug, which Nikolai had taught her to call a *djezve*, glimmered with much polishing. The glass which held the water was polished too, its contents still dancing and settling in the muted light filtering through their blue and red umbrella. The same bright shade kindled the kaleido-

scope peacock-pattern on the tiny brown cups to mysterious new colours. All was as it should be, a gift of the
moment, and already flying as every moment did.

'But such questions are for tomorrow, the next day,
next week.' Nikolai's deep voice cut into her reverie.
'For now, we think only of the next step. Of how we
travel to Kazanlük. . .'

'Not yet,' Mallory interrupted, her mind racing. 'I've
had an idea about what you do with your money.'
Spurred by her blind need to avoid talk of Kazanlük,
she went on quickly, 'Didn't you say Dragalevtsy has a
ski-lift?'

'To the Aleko ski-centre,' he confirmed. 'Our Vitosha
has the best skiing. . .'

'So it must already be a sporty place?'

'Among other things.' The dark eyes regarded her
across the table, immediately catching the direction of
her thoughts. 'You speak of tennis? Yes, I have thought
of teaching it, though not in Dragalevtsy.'

'But it sounds just the place for you to found a tennis
school — an international one,' she argued. 'You'd know
how to publicise it all over the world, and you'd give
your students value for their hard currency.'

'I would also introduce them to beautiful Dragalevtsy
and cultured Sofia,' he rejoined, cautiously pleased.
'And I would keep space for those with talent who
cannot pay.'

'Not too many of those. . .'

'On that, *devoika*, I will make my own decisions.'

'Of course.' She looked down in confusion, the
glowing red of the tablecloth matching the heat she
could feel in her cheeks at her ill-fated attempt to tell
him what to do. 'Sorry.'

'But still,' he added, comforting her, 'I will think
about this idea of yours, *devoika*.'

'Only think about it?' she asked, disappointed. 'I was sure you'd love it.'

'I certainly *like* it. But it is for tomorrow, or next week.' He took a spoonful of water from the glass on the tray, and splashed it over the velvety surface of the coffee. 'For now, we set off to Kazanlük. . .'

'You're doing *my* job on that coffee,' Mallory reproached him.

'Then do it yourself, before it is cold!' But as he handed her the spoon he let his heart-melting smile shine out. 'I like to see the colour lighten as the coffee-grounds sink.'

'I do, too.' She scooped more water with the spoon, and splashed in her turn. 'It's another of the extra little pleasures you get before you start enjoying the taste.'

'Bulgaria is full of such pleasures.'

'I know it.' She watched the paler splashes of water spread and join up over the velvet-dark coffee, signalling that the cold water had pressed the grounds to the bottom of the brew and that it was ready to drink. 'It's a country full and packed down and running over with pleasures, like the bushel measure in the Bible.'

'If we speak of the Bible, I must tell what really happened at the creation of the world,' he announced expansively. 'When the peoples of earth were given their lands, God left none for the Bulgarians. . .'

'Shame!' Mallory put in, responding to the story as he liked her to.

'But it was all right,' he soothed in the way that made it so easy to imagine him telling these stories to his own children. 'God made it up to us by giving us a part of heaven instead.'

'A part of heaven. Yes, that's Bulgaria all right.' She took the *djezve*'s long brass handle, and carefully filled each peacock-patterned cup. 'And after all,' she added, cheered by the fragrance of the dark, rich brew, 'it's not everybody who gets to spend a week in a part of heaven.'

'And the best of our week is yet to come.' He began to unfold the map. 'Tomorrow, in Kazanlük——'

'Coffee?'

'Put it down there.' He indicated the place he wanted it. 'I will drink it soon.'

'You said *I* was letting it get cold.'

'So you were—it should be poured as hot as possible.' However, thus reminded, he took up his cup. 'When we have finished it,' he added, handing her the map, 'we will choose our way together.'

'All right.'

Resigned, she accepted the map and opened it. As ever, she was immediately daunted by its bewildering array of places, all named in a lettering she had only just begun to study and could barely read.

But no, not all. This map, she suddenly realised, held a treasure which had gathered without her noticing. She glanced along the coast at the trail of towns they had visited, each with its name now written again in neat Latin letters. This had been Nikolai's way of helping her find them more easily, and now here they were, every blue-inked name a memory of him. He had written out for her the perfect record of the best few days of all her life, the only few days that had ever mattered.

'I think I like Nesebur best so far.' She studied the blue-inked, Latin-lettered name on the sea next to the near-island town. 'But it's hard to choose. Everywhere's so gorgeous on that coast.'

'Even Burgas?' he queried. 'I think you found it too big and bustling, did you not?'

'It wasn't my absolute favourite,' she admitted. 'But

then, look at the competition! Sozopol, Pomorie, Nessebur, Varna. . .'

She trailed off, unable to put her feelings about them into words. Cobbled streets and white boats and green gardens, shining beaches and comfortable hotels and inviting restaurants, all had run together in her memory as a single, bright perfection. His trail of blue lettering would help her sort it out, but not yet. Soon she might need to live it all again, but for two days she still had the reality, and Nikolai with her to give it meaning.

'You haven't put Madara in yet.' She turned the map to an inland fold. 'I can't see it in your writing anywhere.'

'It is harder inland. I did not wish to write over all the other places around it,' he told her. 'Try and find it for yourself, and we will see if your Cyrillic is now good enough.'

'I don't see why Cyril should have all the credit for this alphabet.' She studied the clear, practical letters which she now knew had been created in the ninth century by two Bulgarian monks.

'Why don't you call it Cyril-and-Methodic?'

'*Haïde!*' he exclaimed with pretended severity. 'You are dodging your test.'

'I'm not, I'm not! I've got Shumen, where we are now.'

She shot him a reproachful glance. The wide street before them was agreeable enough, but they could have eaten in Madara itself, near the great cliff-carved bas-relief of a horseback warrior.

Nikolai wouldn't allow it. They could put in some more mileage before midday, he'd said, and had brought her on to the crossroads town of Shumen. Now they must choose where to go next, and, as far as he was concerned, that simply meant choosing which way to take to Kazanlük.

And even that he'd already settled for himself. 'Find Gabrovo,' he ordered, tacitly releasing her from the task of finding the much smaller Madara, 'and Kazanlük is just after it.'

'Veliko Türnovo's *before* it,' she muttered rebelliously. 'We'll have to drive right past it.'

'We will have time for a quiet moment at the monument of Shipka,' he decided, 'but not for Veliko Türnovo. We cannot do everything in one week, *devoika*.'

'No.' Depressed, she watched him settle the bill. 'I suppose not.'

'Enough of this wishing for what we cannot have.' He pushed back his chair, stood up, and waited for her to join him. 'What we *can* have is the Feast of Roses. You will like it.'

# CHAPTER SEVEN

'Relax, *devoika*!' Nikolai guided the car round another bend. 'I have no plans to drive us over the edge and down the mountain.'

'I know that.' Mallory unclenched her hands with conscious effort. 'And the road's good.'

Too good, her mind chimed in with its own wayward logic. If only we could have a little accident of some kind! Nothing serious, she amended, feeling guiltier than ever. Just enough to keep us here in the mountains until we've missed the Rose Day.

But any accident they might have must come from somewhere other than Nikolai's driving. And her conscience, however uncontrolled, wouldn't let her wish any such troubles on the occasional truck or small family car they overtook, or which passed them in the opposite direction.

'Soon we will be at the Shipka Pass, and through to the other side of the Stara Planina,' he told her soothingly. 'After that, it is no distance to Kazanlük.'

'There's so little traffic.' She spoke too quickly to hide her dismay. 'Are all your roads like this?'

'I told you we had cars.' He slowed for the next bend. 'I did not say we had traffic jams, as in your part of Europe.'

'You needn't blame me for those,' she murmured out of a crotchety need to contradict. '*I* can't even drive.'

'Really not?' He flicked her a surprised sideways glance.

She shrugged. For the last nine years, ever since she

was sixteen, her mother had lectured her about how every woman could and should master the skill of driving. Even now, three years after Mallory's move to London, the arguments came up afresh in each of their rare telephone conversations. Her father agreed, though he never lectured. Instead he pointedly left copies of the Highway Code and driving-school brochures lying about.

'I've a feeling,' Mallory decided, suddenly aware for the first time of the stubborn streak in her own nature, 'that they carried on at me too much. . .'

She broke off, biting her lip. How stupid of her to have spoken so unguardedly now, after a whole five days being careful. Had he noticed?

Of course he had. 'This "they" who carried on at you.' His fine profile stayed cool and distant as a coin-portrait of an emperor. 'You mean your parents, do you not?'

'I. . . I suppose I do,' she admitted numbly.

'So you are ready to. . .' He paused, maybe to take note of the distant obstacle in the straight stretch of road ahead, maybe not. 'To. . .*remember* them?' he ended with studied emphasis.

'*No*!' The word shot from her without her will. 'Not their names, I mean,' she amended lamely. 'Not *my* name. . .'

'Leave it, *devoika*. I think we understand each other.'

She stared ahead, hating her wretched pretence more than ever. Even the amber-pink sunset seemed a reproach, its slanting rays so gloriously beautiful on the ever changing cliffs and crags of the Stara Planina that she felt unfit to be here.

Close up, the obstacle in the road turned out to be a horse-drawn cart trundling noisily on wooden wheels.

The horse, ambling down the crown of the road, stopped when it met them.

'What do we do now?' Mallory asked, her hopes rising. 'Shouldn't we find out who it belongs to?'

'You would ask the horse?'

'Don't tease, Nikolai! It must have wandered away. . .'

'Not at all. But as you are so worried,' he added to her dismay, 'we do this.'

He sounded the lightest possible note on the horn. As if by magic a head popped up in the cart. Impressively capable in working clothes, and still very much in charge of his vehicle, the young man waved a brief return signal, then reined the horse to its own side of the road. Nikolai threw him a smiling comment as they eased past. The man shouted a smiling answer, and gave a backward salute with his whip as they drew away.

'What were you saying?' Mallory demanded, eager as ever to know all she could about Nikolai and his beloved country.

'I asked him why he sleeps at the bottom of his cart on such a road.' Nikolai smiled again at the remembered exchange. 'He said the horse is very wise, and his new wife very—er——' a selective pause '—very *beautiful*. Among other things.'

'What's his new wife got to do with. . .? Oh.' Feeling foolish, Mallory hurried to her next question. 'Is that why the horse had those pretty blue beads on his harness? Because there's just been a wedding?'

'It would have them anyway.' He sounded preoccupied. 'They hold off bad luck.'

'Do they?' she asked, interested. 'I could do with something like that myself. . .'

She choked to an agonised halt. Why must she blurt such things out? Bad enough that Richard might be there ahead of them in Kazanlük, but at least she needn't speak of it, and destroy what perhaps would be the last remaining hours of her happiness.

Luckily, Nikolai understood her differently. Though, heaven knew, his understanding was uncomfortable enough.

'So you still feel they were right, these parents you have. . .forgotten ——' another deliberate pause, while he drove with measured care round the next curve in the road '— to call you by this name you have also forgotten, which means unlucky?'

Mallory breathed deep, and hard. When she finally answered, her voice was as low and controlled as his.

'I've felt very lucky these last few days, Nikolai.'

'I too, *devoika*. I too. And now ——' he drew the car to a halt '— we give thanks for it.'

'What? Oh. . .'

She got out without another word, and walked with him to the great stone monument at the side of the pass. Silent as in a church, they stood where, little more than a hundred years earlier, a vastly outnumbered force of Bulgarians and Russians had held out against the might of the Ottoman Empire and freed the land from its five-hundred-year yoke.

And here, with the hard-won quiet soaking into her, Mallory knew at last that she had to be done with pretending. In this place where so many had given so much, the least she could offer was the truth.

'It's suddenly so clear-cut,' she said when their silent moment was over. 'What these men fought for was right, and what they fought against was wrong.'

'We have other monuments among the mountains, for other battles in this war.' Nikolai spoke softly, yet with a certain urgency. 'And this church ——' he indicated the golden domes far below in the village '—is also a memorial.'

'The very air of this place is a memorial,' she murmured. 'As if their courage had changed it forever. . .' She paused, then turned fully to face him, the wind lifting her hair in the red of sunset. 'And now it's changed *me*, Nikolai.'

'I am glad of that, *devoika*.' He took both her hands, his eyes a dark fire in the sunset. 'It has made you brave enough to tell the truth?'

'I. . .I think so.' She took a gulp of the clean, strong air. 'I. . .I never did lose my memory.' She dared to meet the fire-dark eyes. 'But you know that, don't you?'

He did his side-to-side nod. His hands stayed close and warm round hers, and his eyes, in some way she couldn't understand, held her equally close.

'I *was* confused, at first,' she explained. 'Then everything just. . .happened, and I let it.'

'And you are ready now to be who you are?'

'Oh, *yes*!' the words sprang out, joyous as a fountain. 'That's what you and Bulgaria have done for me—set me free to be myself. Really myself, not. . .' The fountain ceased, and only her new courage sustained her. 'Not who I used to be.' She couldn't meet his eyes any more, but instead had to look down at their linked hands. 'I don't *like* who I used to be, Nikolai.'

'Yet that is you also.' His hands kept their steadfast grip. 'You must accept this other you, even though you do not like her.'

'Yes. It's all so clear, up here with you. But——' she let her gaze slide sideways to the uncompromising stone squareness of the monument '—I'm not that strong yet.'

'You will be soon? You must be, *devoika*.' His hands lifted hers urgently. 'Very soon.'

'I will be, very soon. I promise.'

'And I promise to help all I can.'

And here it was again, the same exchange of vows she had sensed between them when they had first come ashore at Duni. But these vows were more serious, and not only because they had been made in this hallowed place. This time they were spoken aloud, out on the thyme-scented air for both to understand.

And did she understand? She wasn't sure. When Nikolai released one of her hands, and led her back to the car by the other, she had the strongest feeling that he had been testing her, and that the testing wasn't over yet.

'One thing more, *devoika*.' He had opened her door, but wouldn't release her to get into it. 'This other you that you cannot yet face. She had no husband?'

'Oh course not!' Mallory stared in astonishment. 'How could you need to ask? I told you I was a virgin. . .'

'And at that time I believed you.'

'And n-now you don't?' She could hardly bear to say it.

He shrugged. 'You are very beautiful. There must have been men. . .'

'And seeing I lied about my memory, why not about that?' she interrupted, close to tears.

'I would not say it like this, but yes.' The deep voice was cool, keeping distance between them. 'One or many of these men could have——' his hand tightened like a vice '—could have taken you to bed.'

'I can only say they didn't.' She gulped, and raised her face pleadingly. 'Truly not.'

The fire-dark eyes burnt into hers. 'Not one?'

'Not one.'

A tear escaped as she spoke, and ran down her cheek. She tried to shake it away, but the movement only let out the gasping sniffle she'd hoped to suppress. She grabbed up her bag and pretended to search it for a handkerchief, knowing she had none. She was trying not to sniffle again when he took the bag from her, and dropped it who knew where.

Then his arms were round her, and his lips tasting the wetness on her cheek. They slid to her mouth, and she met them with a delight that had something of reverence. It would have been easy to kiss greedily, to take as much of each other as they could get after five days of denial, but she sensed how he was reining in his appetite, and could only suppress her own. This was the start of something new between them. His gentle mouth on hers recognised that, and so did her gentle response.

Released once more into the flaring sunset, she looked up at him. 'Must we go to Kazanlük, Nikolai?'

'We must, *devoika*, if only because you are afraid of what you will find there.' He paused. 'I do not know what you fear, but I know you must face it.'

'Yes.' She bowed her head, ashamed of this last attempt to run away. 'Here we go, then.' She took one more deep breath of the mountain air. 'Wait a minute. . .' She inhaled again, and turned to Nikolai. 'Do I smell roses?'

'It could be,' he agreed. 'The name Shipka means "wild rose". The roses here were always known for their fragrance.' He inhaled in his turn. 'The scent is there, is it not? Perhaps it comes up from the valley ——'

'It's a sign,' Mallory interrupted, and filled her lungs, her mind, her senses with the haunting fragrance. 'Let's go,' she urged with that new, special courage she had learnt here in this special country. 'It's going to be all right.'

And perhaps it would be. The scent of roses grew ever stronger, and she found herself ever more relaxed as they dropped into the soft air of the valley. Presently they drove between magical acres of waist-high bushes, all spangled with pink folded buds and all yielding their swooning fragrance to a sky luminous with the rose-coloured afterglow of the vanished sun.

'This is the strongest their perfume will ever be,' Nikolai told her, amused by her rapturous sniffing. 'After tomorrow, all that scent goes into baskets, and then into bottles.'

'They can't take it *all*,' Mallory objected. 'There has to be some left in the air.'

'There is, but we take all we can. It needs two thousand roses to make one gram of oil. . .'

'Goodness! It must be pretty valuable stuff, then?'

'Weight for weight, more precious than gold.' He changed gear with a brief, sardonic laugh. 'That's a lot of hard currency you're sniffing, *devoika*.'

'Then it must be quite the most romantic hard currency in the world,' she retorted, and sniffed again.

By the time they reached Kazanlük she was almost drunk with the perfume. Could that be why she felt so free, so fearless, so ready to enjoy herself? No, it was more than that. Enjoyment was in the air of this prosperous little town, given off by every bright-clad individual promenading the garlanded streets.

'The embroidery!' she exclaimed as a group of girls drifted through the perfumed air on her side of the car. 'On the aprons, the sleeves, the skirts, the bodices. . .'

'And now you see how a Bulgarian man should dress,' Nikolai put in as another resplendent group crossed the road before them. 'Everything he wears should be made with love, by his own woman.'

'Isn't that rather a tall order?' She thought of the rose-russet shirt in her flight-bag, hand-embroidered, but not by the wife who had given it to him. 'Didn't you say they even spin and weave the cloth? So these outfits must take several lifetimes.'

'Exactly.' He did his side-to-side nod at the wheel. 'They come down from father to son, mother to daughter.'

The hotel was crowded when they reached it, but Nikolai had long since booked the rooms, which now only had to be claimed. After the interlude on Shipka, Mallory's conscience troubled her more than usual about her illegal passport, but the man at the desk as usual accepted it with only a brief '*Merci*' and went on chatting to Nikolai. Waiting for them to finish, she snuffed up the lemony scent of the yellow roses in the peacock-patterned vase on the polished desk.

'What were you talking about?' she asked, inquisitive as ever, when they had accepted their keys and moved on.

Nikolai guided her through the rose-decorated foyer, and up the rose-decorated staircase. 'I wished to know if they had any other English people staying here, or expected.'

'Oh.' Dry-mouthed, she froze among the cascading roses on the landing. 'And. . .are there any?'

'None, *devoika*.'

'None at all?'

'Not one. But of course —— ' the dark eyes held hers ' — there are plenty of other places to stay.'

'Still. . .' She left the thought unfinished on a new rush of optimism. 'I really am going to enjoy this, Nikolai.'

And she did, every moment of it. She ate little supper, but only because she was so impatient to be out in the eve-of-carnival streets. They managed it only just in time. The promenading crowds had already thinned when they reached the scent-laden, rose-resplendent gardens of the place whose name Nikolai resoundingly translated as the Institute of the Oleaginous Rose, Essential Oils and Medicinal Plants.

'Suddenly there's far fewer of those gorgeous embroidered costumes about,' Mallory commented as she finished the rose-flavoured ice-cream he had bought for her from a street-vendor. 'Where is everybody?'

'Sleeping while they can, I think.' Nikolai indicated their way. 'Everything has to start early here. Tomorrow they begin the real picking at first light.'

'First *light*?' Remembering how early it came, she gazed at him in mock-dismay. 'Not even at sunrise?'

'It must be over by then. The sun must not shine on the open petals; it dries the perfume.' He swooped on her, and, before she could dodge, licked a stray dab of ice-cream from the side of her mouth. 'You taste of roses, *devoika*. Roses and yourself. . .' His smile faded. 'Perhaps I should not have done that.'

Mallory could only stare up at the black and gold darkness of him in the yellow light of the street-lamps. Her whole being seemed to have rushed to the brief contact, and the place he had touched now pulsed its message to the rest of her like some dark inner beacon. Seeking distraction, she found the last of her ice-cream melting in her hand. She had trouble swallowing it, but its chill brought her to herself.

'Don't you like the taste, then?' she asked maliciously.

'It is exquisite,' he murmured through the dimness. 'I had forgotten for a moment that it is forbidden.'

'And. . .must it stay forbidden?' The question dragged from her almost against her will. 'Isn't it time we. . .tasted?'

'I wish to do more than taste, *devoika*.' He faced her

in the near-dark of the ever quieter street. 'I wish to hold and keep. And this I will not do with a woman who has no name.'

It was as if a thorn had pierced her among all the roses. He didn't trust her yet. And why should he, when she wouldn't talk about herself?

I'm Mallory Hawthorne. She moved her lips soundlessly, trying to form the words in the friendly, rose-scented near-dark. Twenty-five years old. I came here with a man who turned out to be married. . .

Exactly. How could she admit to being so foolish? And if she did, who could blame Nikolai for suspecting that she had been worse than foolish?

But I walked into the sea, she argued inside her head. As soon as I found out, I tried to get away. . .'

No use. That made it worse, not better. She should have stayed and faced her troubles, instead of trying to run away from them. She could see that clearly now, but it didn't help. How could she acknowledge such cowardice, here in this land of heroes? Why, she positively hated the pathetic creature she had been. . .

A gentle touch on the back of her waist brought her to herself. She jumped, and looked up to the black and gold shadow which was Nikolai.

'Come, *devoika*.' He drew her along with him. 'Let us think only of now.'

And as they strolled back to the hotel he talked only of the Valley of Roses, or Rosova Dolina. How its sheltered climate south of the Balkan Range supplied three-quarters of the world's rose-oil. How the precious oil was distilled from rose-water, and this also used to flavour liqueurs and fine confectionery. How another kind of Bulgarian hero, the peasant Bai Ganyou, had set forth with his saddle-bags full of tiny bottles of rose-oil, and made it famous among perfume-makers everywhere.

That night Mallory dreamt of roses, and after the dreams slept deeply. When Nikolai knocked on her door, she thought at first that she'd only been in bed for a minute or two. Then she remembered their agreement not to miss the opening ceremony, and scrambled into her clothes by lamplight. Still half asleep, she met him in the corridor, and in a velvet dimness lightened in the east with the grey silk of morning, they joined the crowds making for the rose-fields.

'The desk-clerk gave me these,' Nikolai murmured as the perfume grew ever more heady. 'Take one.'

'Whatever for?' She looked down in bewilderment at the two small safety-pins.

'You will see.'

And she did, almost at once. A blazingly beautiful girl welcomed them, a chaplet of roses on her head and a basket of roses at her feet. While Mallory wondered at her superbly embroidered blouse and bolero, full skirt and brilliant apron, she raised her arms in their wide, white, embroidered sleeves, and tucked a rose behind Mallory's ear.

Now it was Nikolai's turn. Mallory stiffened as these two splendid creatures faced each other, but the girl only smiled up at him, down at the rose, and sideways at the watchful young man, equally gorgeously costumed and with a rose already tucked behind his ear, who lingered near. Then she offered Nikolai his rose with a graceful little bow, and moved on to the next guest.

'You see?' Nikolai flourished his pin. 'Now we can be sure not to lose them. Come here.'

She wonderingly obeyed, and he pinned his rose to the breast of her crocus-blue shirt. She stood helpless as ever under his hands and drank in his nearness, the maleness of him between her and the lightening sky.

'Wake up, *devoika*!'

'Hmm? Oh. . .' She found him about to take her own rose from her, and quickly held it away. 'No, let me.'

Without waiting for an answer, she fixed it to the dark waistcoat he wore as ever with dark trousers and white shirt. When she felt his hands either side of her waist she almost stabbed herself with the pin, but at last the job was done, the two roses nestling between them as he bent and kissed her cheek.

'Now we have exchanged roses,' he murmured in her ear as he straightened. 'Perhaps that also is a sign.'

She didn't dare ask what sort of sign he was looking for. Anyway, she felt she knew, and treasured his rose at her breast through all of that glouriofs day.

The girls soon left their gift-rose baskets for another kind, wide and shallow with a soaring arc of a handle. Then men and girls began a slow dance to the intricate rhythms and harmonies of their own singing. The song ended in the transparent hush of morning, the light ever stronger, and the first roses of the harvest were plucked and laid in the baskets. Then the sun was up, and it was time to go back to breakfast.

'Rose-flavoured *jam*?' Mallory queried, tasting it.

'On this day, what else? Not too long now, *devoika* —— ' Nikolai divided the last of the fruit juice between their two glasses ' — or we will miss the start of the parade.'

But they didn't miss the start of the parade, or any moment of it. They heard the accordion band, and the resplendently uniformed army band, and the band made up of bagpipes and flutes and mandolines, which Nikolai said were traditional instruments. They saw the drum majorettes, and the rose-decked floats of dancers, and

the weirdly masked figures with cattle bells on their
belts, who leapt aggressively to the beating of a drum,
and the man dressed for some reason as a rose-crowned
bride, and the line of children being a railway train, and
the dancing pantomime horse, and, at last, the Rose
Queen on her garlanded throne. And when it had all
gone by they followed where it led, to the huge tents
where even the scent of roses was defeated by the
savoury aromas of food and wine.

'*Blagodaria*.' Mallory smiled at the girl who poured
rose-water over her hands, though she couldn't smell it
any more. 'I'm hungry,' she told Nikolai as they shook
their hands dry.

'It is time to eat,' he confirmed, and led her to where
the food was being served. 'I promised you *shishkebab*,
remember?'

The luscious skewered meat from the charcoal grill,
though only a tiny part of the banquet on offer, was
more than enough. With it they had a wine Nikolai
called Trakia, and after it a piece of rose-flavoured
Turkish delight. Then they begged more rose-water to
wash their hands, and made for the stalls where the
craftsmen had laid out their goods.

'*Ne, blagodaria*,' Mallory had to say over and over
again as she was offered beautiful embroidery or gleam-
ing copperware. '*Ne*. . . How do I say I've no money,
Nikolai?'

'I have enough——'

'No!' she cut in, so quickly and gracelessly that she
had to explain. 'I mean, no, thank you, I've no room to
carry anything.'

No room, no strength, no name. The words hung in
the air between them, unspoken yet all-pervading. She
flung her head back in relief at the nearby sound of
musicians tuning up.

'Can we go and watch the dancing?'

'Better than that.' He took her hand. 'We dance also.'

'What, the *horo*?' She hung back, appalled at the idea of herself in one of the athletic, complicated chain-dances they had watched together. 'I don't know how!'

'It is not a *horo* but a *rûchenitsa*, a couple dance,' he corrected her. 'For this we improvise.'

'Improvise?' she echoed as they approached the dance-floor and found only one couple on it. 'With these experts?'

'We will have our turn; you will see.'

Relieved to have it postponed, Mallory settled to watch the man and woman who were dancing. Each held an embroidered kerchief, and wove patterns in the air while they met and parted, met again and danced a little way together. Presently the woman fled and the man followed, then she turned to face him but still retreated backwards, all to the lively, foot-tapping rhythms of the dance. He circled her like a hunter, and, when he had her captive in one place with her kerchief above her head, put on a display of ever more vigorous leaps and kicks until at last she gave him her hands and they circled the floor together.

'Now we can begin.' Nikolai took Mallory's hand, and urged her out with him.

Much to her relief they were quickly surrounded by dancers, each, as far as she could see, doing his or her own thing. And she didn't have to be noticeable — in this dance at least; that was for the men. She knew that her own heel-and-toe bounce was over-simple compared to the graceful pivoting of the women round her, but she could keep to the rhythm and presently even enjoy it. Nikolai meanwhile circled her and stamped, dropped to one knee and the other, snapped his fingers and flourished his handkerchief and shouted until, exhausted, she offered him her hands. Even then he didn't stop, but circled the floor with her, took her to the side, and left her there while he went on dancing.

From her place by the edge, she watched the other women give up one by one. At last only men were left, and ever fewer, until it was only Nikolai and two others in an exuberant triangle, each trying to outdance the others. The faster the music the higher and wider the leaps, until the musicians themselves gave up, and brought the display to an end with a final defiant chord to a round of applause from the onlookers.

'That was absolutely marvellous,' Mallory greeted Nikolai as he rejoined her. 'You were the best of the lot. . .'

'Only here,' he disclaimed with his usual arrogant modesty, and mopped his forehead with the handkerchief. 'I would not have been the best in Dragalevtsy.'

'I bet you would.'

But at the mention of his home, a sudden chill descended on her in the heated, scented air. When they had first come ashore, he had been determined to take her to his family. Did he still want to, knowing so clearly of her deceit? And if he didn't, what was to become of her? '*Think only of now*', he'd told her, but that *now* was nearly over. Tomorrow the roses would all be picked.

'I have lost a button.' He held up one wrist, loose-cuffed, then rolled back the sleeves from his powerful tanned forearms. 'But anyway, I must change this shirt.'

'Can I sew the button back for you?' she asked eagerly as they left the tent. 'Can I, Nikolai?'

'If we can find one to match,' he answered, laughing. 'So our *rûchenitsa* has tamed you to your woman's tasks, *devoika*?'

'What? Oh. . .' She remembered how the men had danced the women into submission. 'Certainly not!'

But he was right. She wanted to take that hot, crumpled shirt from him and lovingly wash and iron it. She wanted to polish his shoes for him, and put his clothes on a hanger every night when he took them off. . .

'Hear the singing!' he exclaimed as they came within range of the tuneful, sophisticated harmonies. 'We have sent many great singers to the opera-houses of the world, but plenty are left. . .'

The hours passed like drifts of rose-petals. Soon, too soon, their pinned roses drooped with thirst, and it was evening.

'I must change before we eat,' Nikolai observed as they strolled back to the hotel.

'I don't want to eat.' Mallory spoke dreamily, and yet with mounting dread. 'I don't want anything but just to walk with you like this to the end of the world.'

But before ever the world ended, her plane would be leaving without her. Tomorrow afternoon it would take off, and the next morning, when she didn't return to work, the questions would be asked, the trail followed. . .

But she still had tonight. Tonight, in honour of this last, perfect day, she would put aside her travel clothes and for the first time wear the other garment she had chosen at the Villa Lamia. Back in her room, showered and refreshed and with her rose reviving in a glass of water, she drew the plum-purple sweater-dress from where it had lain until now at the bottom of her bag.

As she hoped, it shook out uncreased. And here was the matching make-up—purple varnish for her finger and toe-nails and purple lipstick for her full mouth. The colour suited her, she was glad to note. That left only the glittery purple shadow for her tilted eyelids, and then she could slip her feet into the glitter-heeled sandals, ease the dress over her new-washed hair, and be just in time to open the door to Nikolai's double knock.

'Are you hungry, *devoika*. . .?' He stopped abruptly, then stepped in and closed the door, his eyes unreadable as dark stones. 'This is one of the Villa Lamia designs, is it not?'

'You. . .you don't like it?' she faltered. 'I picked the plainest I could find. . .oh, my goodness!' She stared into the mirror by the door. 'I'd no idea it came so low,' she admitted, pinching together the swooping V-neck.

'Or so high?' His coal-dark glance swept down to her mid-thigh hem, and up again. 'And this——' he nodded to where she still held her neckline together '—only makes it worse.'

'What? But how can it. . .?'

She saw that he was right. The purple rib clung even to the hollow of her navel. On either side of the held-togther neckline her breasts pointed high and proud through the stretched material.

She hastily dropped her hand, but it didn't help. The coal-dark gaze was already on fire, and the fire held her captive. Slowly, as if against his will, his hands rose to her bare arms, smoothed them from elbow to shoulder, and gripped hard, claiming her body for his pleasure. She gasped, and closed her eyes on the turmoil within her, and waited for whatever he should do next.

And after all, he did nothing but leave her with all her longings unappeased. She heard a choked exclamation, felt the loss of his hands, and knew that he was brushing lightly past her into the room beyond. She couldn't believe it, couldn't bear it, but at last had to open her eyes, and found him shaking out her discarded tulip-patterned skirt.

'I like this better,' he announced curtly.

She accepted it from him without a word, and changed quickly in the bathroom. At least she didn't have to put on the tired blue shirt. The hotel laundry had washed and ironed the yellow one to new crispness, and once it was on she felt reasonably fresh after all. When she rejoined Nikolai with the purple dress bundled in her hands, his opaque severity melted a little.

'Give that to me.' He took the dress from her. 'This is what we do with the serpent-women who eat children.' He flung it across the room.

'I. . .I didn't know it was going to look like that. I suppose I should have tried it on. . .' She stared to where it had fallen, a curled poisonous thing by the wall. 'I only wanted to make this evening special.' She raised her head, and found she was having to blink away the tears to see him better. 'After our beautiful day. . .'

'Our beautiful day is not ended yet.' Suddenly he was brisk, and practical, and all kindness. 'You need food, *devoika*.' He offered his arm in its fresh, crisp white sleeve. 'They tell me there is a very good *mehana* by the station. . .'

Her tears swallowed back, she moved along the corridor with him, and down the stairs. Oh, the height of him, her heart sang, the girder-spare shoulders and shield-hard chest, the defiant profile and springy hair!

The hotel lobby was crowded. Nikolai spoke of some special group performing here this evening, but she hardly heard, still spellbound by the warmth of him, the muscular arm here for her to lean on, the strength and wisdom and kindness which had never failed her in all the five days she had known him. . .

'Mallory!'

'Yes?'

She had responded to her name before she knew it, before even she recognised the familiar baritone voice. Only when she dragged her eyes from Nikolai to the square, country-solid figure before them did she realise what she had done, what had happened.

'Richard!'

# CHAPTER EIGHT

IN THAT frozen moment, a series of incoherent thoughts tumbled through Mallory's brain.

He's been drinking. He looks as if he hasn't slept for a week. He's cut himself shaving. And where's his *swagger* gone?

The last took her by surprise, because she hadn't known Richard swaggered at all. But he did; she could see it now even though it wasn't there any more.

That's silly, was her next thought, to be seeing something that isn't there.

But it was, in the fancy dress. For heaven's sake, why a green suede tunic, of all things? His shirt was a paler shade of the same forest-green, and so were the jeans tucked in his pointy-toed green boots. The felt hunting-hat dangling from one of his hands was dark green, with a strange pointy brim.

'Wh-why the leprechaun outfit?' She found to her surprise that she was voicing her rambling thoughts aloud. 'All you need is the crock of gold. . .'

She broke off. Richard's cheeks, more florid than she remembered, had flushed with rage, and his free hand balled into a fist which drew back as if to let fly.

How could I ever have fancied him? There went her wayward thoughts again.

For a split second she relived the unpleasant party where she'd met him. It had been given by one of the showy, empty men she hated but couldn't seem to help attracting. This one called himself an agent, whatever that meant. She'd gone along out of sheer loneliness, but, from the moment she'd stepped over the writhing couple in the hall, had wished she'd stayed at home. Soon a drunken guest had been trying to wrestle her to the carpet, until tweed-clad Richard had shouldered him away and taken her home.

On that evening he'd seemed a breath of fresh air. Now, heavy-eyed and reeking of alcohol and nicotine, he had become a different person.

'I've been out of my mind with worry,' he grated over that menacing fist. 'And all the time, it was only that you——' his bloodshot eyes veered up to Nikolai's detached frown, and returned to Mallory '——you found a proposition you liked better. . .'

'Mr Sherwood, I presume?'

Nikolai's deep voice smoothly took charge. His ember-dark gaze, still unreadable, fixed itself on the doubled fist. Richard tried to outface him, but presently he too had to look down at the fist, and slowly let it drop unclenched to his side.

Satisfied, Nikolai moved his stiff-haired, dominant head towards Mallory. 'And this lady travelled here as your wife?'

'She's no lady,' Richard muttered. 'And I didn't shell out her fare just so she could have a high old time with you.'

'As it is important to you——' Nikolai didn't bother to hide his contempt '——I will return the money.'

'Thanks, I'll take it. It's only right——'

'I'll pay it myself.' It wasn't what Mallory had meant to say, but at least it put an end to this sordid money-talk. 'I suppose you need every penny you can get,' she added to Richard, 'with a wife and three young children to support.'

His loose mouth dropped open. 'How the hell do you——?'

'A wife? Children?' Nikolai's frown gathered weight. 'This man is married, with a family?'

'He certainly is.' She flicked a bitter glance at the oddly dressed two-timer who had once convinced her he was a caring person. 'Their youngest is eighteen months old.'

The ember-dark eyes fixed hers. 'You knew this?'

'Yes. . . No!' She gazed up in dismay, desperate to put right the damaging impression she had given. 'I mean——'

'Of course I'm married!' Richard was now bent on justifying himself. 'I never said I wasn't.'

And he probably never did, not straight out, she realised with a distant contempt. All he did was act like a single man, and let me believe he was one.

But she couldn't spare a glance for Richard. Her eyes were all for Nikolai, and the new, frightening heat slowly building behind that cool façade.

'As if my being married would make any difference to this little groupie here——'

'This *what*?' Mallory gasped. 'Have you gone mad?'

'Groupie,' Nikolai repeated with a frozen calm she did not recognise. 'That is what they called the foolish women who followed me from match to match.'

'Well, this one used to follow me from gig to gig.' Richard jerked his head at Mallory. 'She went to bed with my agent, just to be asked to the party he was giving for me.'

Outraged, Mallory faced him. 'How can you say such things? I hardly knew the man. . .'

'When did that ever stop you?'

'But I never even went out with him,' she found herself pleading, helpless against these monstrous lies. 'I only met him when he c-came to the bank for financial advice.'

'And you advised him all right, with trimmings,' the braying tones stated with absolute conviction. 'Which got you as far as my drummer. . .'

'Your what?' Maybe she'd wake up in a minute.

'Don't tell me you've forgotten how we met?' Richard put on a hateful parody of looking sentimentally into her eyes. 'When I hauled you off old Roger——'

'You did *not*!' The sense of nightmare thickened. 'What is all this about agents and drummers? You're a farmer, aren't you?'

'Some of the time.' Shuffling, he indicated the guitar by him on the table. 'The rest, I'm——'

'Robin Hood, folk-singer.' Nikolai read the name aloud from a nearby poster.

'But that's all wrong, isn't it?' she objected, nightmarishly confused by the detail. 'It was Allen-a-Dale who sang. . .'

'Allen-a-Dale was our lead guitar, until we split.' Richard's unease deepened, as if reminded of something else he needed to justify. 'Old Roger went too — that's Will Scarlett. . .'

'Who wore scarlet?' Mallory suppressed a hysterical giggle.

'We got lots of bookings,' Richard asserted furiously, then checked himself. 'But I'm doing fine without them, just fine.'

'Even though you are well down the bill?' Nikolai put in, distant and chilly.

Mallory shot him a grateful glance. Did he realise how paralysed she'd been by these vile accusations? Was he speaking to give her a breathing-space? Certainly for the moment he had stemmed Richard's venom, the lies forgotten in favour of self-serving ambition.

'Oh, I know I'm not all that famous *yet*. But I'm going

to be, just you wait.' The bleary eyes narrowed, the loose mouth thinned to a mean slash. 'I'll show them all. . .'

'So you change partners the way you change women?'

Mallory was astonished to hear her own voice so quiet and composed. Perhaps her time with Nikolai had taught her more than she knew. She shot him another grateful glance, but the dark eyes stonily resisted hers, and she had to look away quickly to keep up her new-found courage.

'You're a fine one to talk!' Richard turned to her, his grievance surfacing once more. 'You sneak away from me —'

'And you —' her voice suddenly had all the strength it needed to cut through the coarse tones ' — don't bother to find out what's become of me.'

'Why should I, when you're all cosied up to lover-boy here?'

'You didn't know that. I might. . .' Mallory faltered, recovered, and brought it out cold as steel. 'I might have been dead, for all you knew.'

'But you weren't; you were trying the local stuff —'

'Be careful, Mr Sherwood.' Nikolai's smoke-dark eyes had flared dangerously.

Richard was heavy, aggressive, and drunk enough to ignore such warnings. His only reaction was to throw another scornful jerk of his head at Mallory. 'You're the one who should be careful, mate, mixed up with that little cat. God knows where she's been.'

'How dare you say such things?' Mallory faced him at her full five feet two inches. 'You know they're not true.'

'So you're coming the innocent, are you?' The blood-shot eyes stared opaquely into hers. 'You haven't let on till now that you sleep around with married men and know you're doing it?'

'I didn't know, and if I had —— '

'You know it all, babe! Every trick in the book.' Richard turned once more to Nikolai. 'You're giving her it rough, I hope? That's how she likes it —— '

'I told you to be careful, Mr Sherwood.' Nikolai's silky whisper tore through the crudeness like a well-honed blade. 'You have said all I wish to hear.'

'Oh, well, I'd better stop then, hadn't I?' Richard retorted. 'I'd better leave you to hump your little slut in peace —— '

The stream of abuse ended abruptly in a horrible, cracking thud. Mallory blinked, wondering how she could have failed to see the blow. All she'd been aware of was Nikolai's icy profile, the girder shoulders swinging almost casually sideways, the sinewy arm flexing past her. Presumably the power-packed fist had landed exactly where he meant it to.

'You've knocked him out,' she exclaimed as the square, green-clad figure crumpled to the floor like a bag of dirty washing.

'Quiet, *dev*. . .' He swallowed back his name for her, and dusted off his hands with icy, disturbing calm. 'He called you Mallory, did he not?'

She stared back at him, unable to speak.

'Mallory, the unlucky one,' he went on with an air of detached interest. 'Mal, the evil one.'

'I was going to tell you, honest!' she burst out. 'I was only waiting until our perfect day was over. . .'

'Our. Perfect. Day.' The deep voice gave back the words without expression. 'Yes, it is over now.'

He turned to where the desk-clerk was pushing through the murmuring, interested onlookers. Mallory

glanced down at Richard, and saw to her immense relief
that he was fingering his chin and muttering thickly.

'If your boyfriend's broken anything I'll sue.'

The onlookers parted again, this time to let through a
splendidly costumed woman with a glass of water. The
moment she appeared a costumed man took the glass,
dropped to one knee, cradled the heavy shoulders from
the ground with one arm, and fed water to his self-
appointed charge sip by sip.

'I'm all right,' Richard grumbled after the second sip.
'Let me up.' He struggled to free himself, water spilling
over his Robin Hood tunic. 'Get this do-gooder off me,
will you?'

The do-gooder grinned disarmingly at Mallory. 'He is
item before us in show. Must be well to sing.' His eyes
sought the guitar, checked over it, and looked up again
in relief. 'Is good that this is not broken, like his own
was, in last fight. . .'

Mallory didn't hear the rest. She was aware of the
desk-clerk stepping in, but that voice also receded
quickly into the distance. Nikolai had grabbed one of
her wrists and was marching her across the lobby, back
the way they had come.

'What are you doing?' she protested, stumbling as he
dragged her after him up the stairs.

He didn't answer, just hauled her up and stormed on.
She stumbled again on the top step, and this time he
whirled to her.

'Can you not stay on your feet, unlucky one?'

'Y-you were g-going too fast for me. . .'

She trailed off. It was all she could do not to cower
away from the pent-up fury in that livid face. The colour
over the high cheekbones had drained to an olive pallor
which made the stiffly upright hair seem coal-black. His
mouth was no more than a dark line, and his eyes under

the straight, cinder-black eyebrows like twin gateways
to hell.

'P-please, Nikolai!' she quavered. 'I know you're
angry — you have the right to be angry — but — — '

She got no further. Without a word he put both hands
on her waist and swung her up to him, clamped her
slightness roughly to his side with her feet dangling, and
hurtled them both along the corridor in sprinter's
strides.

'But wh-where are we *going*?' she couldn't help
asking, though she wouldn't have dared struggle.
'What's *happening*. . .?'

No answer, just his arm holding her so tight that she
could feel the thundering of his heart.

She tried again. 'This is crazy, Nikolai. Think what
we must look like!'

If he cared about that he didn't say so, and she gave
up. After all, it was good to be so close to him, close and
sheltered by his angry strength. She took deep breaths
of him, of roses and cinnamon and roused, fighting
male, and was almost sorry when he dumped her on her
feet at the door of her room.

'Wh-what?' She stared stupidly at his demanding
hand, thrust out palm upward. 'What do you want. . .?
Oh.'

She fished her key from her pocket. He opened the
door, bundled her in, pressed in after her, and banged
the door shut on them both. Then he took her by the
shoulders and stared down at her, hot-eyed in the fading
day, his fingers digging into her flesh through the yellow
shirt.

'And now, Mallory,' he murmured, barely above a
whisper, 'you will tell me your full name.'

'It's Hawthorne.' She flinched from the banked-down
anger, but had no thought of disobedience. 'I'm Mallory

Hawthorne.' Here it came, the little speech she had already tried and failed to make. 'Twenty-five years old. I came here —— '

'You came here as the wife of the buffoon we have just left,' he cut in as if he couldn't bear to hear her say it. 'So that is what Mallory Hawthorne likes.'

'N-not any more. . .'

'So let us see what else she likes.'

He twisted his fingers into her hair and pulled cruelly, tilting her face up to his. Then he clamped his mouth on hers, silencing her shocked protest and punishing her with his lips.

The punishment only lasted a moment. Rebelling from their tasks, his hands and mouth quickly went their own way. His fingers released her hair and instead explored her scalp, then slid on with loving care to caress her ear, her cheek, her jaw. His mouth tasted each of her willing lips in turn, and, when she let her tongue steal out, tasted that too with infinite gentleness. At last with a stifled exclamation he gathered her to him. Their next kiss was long and ecstatic, a kiss of pure joy which must have been waiting to happen to them since the world began.

The rest went fast. She undid her clothes with fierce haste, letting them lie where they fell. She wanted every moment of him, from the very first when those tanned girder shoulders, that shield-hard chest emerged dark and powerful from his white shirt.

But already, by the time she was able to look up at him, he was naked. He had cast away his clothes as quickly as she had, and pulled the covers from the bed. The confusion of different textures swirled dark and light round his feet like sea-foam round an emerging god as he stayed for a moment with his back to her, busy in some way she did not understand.

'But presently he turned to face her, and she could drink in the dark perfection of him. The wide, hair-sprinkled chest, vibrant with health, narrowed to a hard, flat belly where another triangle of hair led her greedy eye naturally to. . .

'Oh, my goodness!' she murmured, astonished by her first real-life close-up view of what happened when a man wanted a woman. 'And. . .and you're wearing a. . .'

'There will be no unwanted child.' He didn't glance down.

'Wh-What's the matter?' she faltered, chilled by the harsh tones. 'You surely aren't thinking about what Richard——?'

'Enough, Mallory Hawthorne.'

And then all speech was at an end, and all thought too. The moment he scooped her into his arms, set her on the bed, and covered her, she was swallowed up entirely by such feelings as she had never known before. When his hard mouth took hers she gave it freely, and rejoiced in the mingling of his hot, hard limbs with hers. When his hard, muscular body pressed her to the sheet, she surged up to him with all her own feminine power, her yielding softness welcoming his hardness.

She never knew whether it was his movement or hers which parted her thighs. It didn't matter; nothing mattered but this tremendous moment when at last they were one, and she could cry out with the pain and pleasure of it.

'I hurt you,' he murmured against her cheek, resting within her. 'I am too quick for you.'

'No. . . *No!*' she breathed, her week-long hunger hot upon her through the trifling pain. 'Go on. *Please go on!*'

And he went on, smooth and hot and strong and

sweet. She accepted him, moved against him, treasured the male push of him with her answering female pull, and wondered at the pleasure which only a man — only this man — could bring her. The pleasure gathered in her like the tide, swung her towards the moon, rocked her among the stars, whirled her to the end of time. . .

And was over. And time hadn't ended after all, though the day had. Darkness lowered at the window, feebly yellowed by the street-lamps, and Nikolai wasn't staying with her to kiss and murmur, but rising and leaving her. His shadow moved with that loved, springy, athlete's walk to close the curtains, then crossed to the wall-switch and put on the top light.

Mallory flinched in the white glare. 'Do we need that?'

He didn't answer or even look in her direction. By now he had turned his back full on her, and was kneeling in all his superb nakedness to the tangle of fabric on the floor, separating his garments from the bedclothes. Even in this humble task he was so gloriously handsome that Mallory had to catch her breath.

'When you first undressed you looked like a sea-god,' she murmured timidly, rising on one elbow the better to view his splendid back. 'Now you look like a sea-god sorting out his laundry. . . Oh, my goodness!' She exclaimed as he rose and turned towards her. 'Can you really want me again so soon?'

'I have wanted you ever since I first touched you in the water days ago.' He hastily turned his back on her again. 'Such wanting is what I live with.'

Nevertheless, when he next faced her he was wearing his trousers. He was also carrying the sheet he had pulled from the bed, and advancing to where she lay without a single glance down at her own nakedness. She felt the sheet drop lightly over her, hiding her from his view, and then he was gone, bundling the rest of his clothes under one arm and striding towards the bathroom.

'What are you doing, Nikolai?' she called after him in dismay. 'Why don't you. . .?'

She had to stop there, because she didn't know what she wanted from him. She only knew that this stony march away from her, this air of being about to get on with his life as if she'd never existed, wasn't it.

Only when his bare, high-arched foot met some coiled darkness on the floor did he pause, to stoop to it. He rose with one arm out, the purple dress held between finger and thumb like something poisonous.

'You should wear this after all. It is just right for you.'

'It isn't!' she choked, holding back her tears. 'I'm not a serpent-woman. I'm not, I'm not. . .'

But she was talking to herself. He only spread his hand fastidiously, dropped the despised garment, and went on into the bathroom. Very quickly, the noise of the shower made it clear that he was washing away all traces of her.

Disowning me. He believes everything Richard said about me, she thought, her own anger slowly catching fire. He's taken the word of that drunken lout without asking for my side of it.

She pushed away the sheet he had put over her, and swung her legs to the floor. Ignoring the new little aches the movement set up within her, she padded over to the purple dress. Its colour seemed repulsively livid in the overhead light, but what did that matter now? She already had it on her finger-nails anyway.

Seeing he's branded me a serpent-woman, I've nothing to lose by wearing this, she thought drearily as she pulled the dress over her head. At least it'll cover me.

Her long hair caught under the collar. She yanked it out and shook it away from her, then gathered up her crumpled clothes, put them on a hanger, and unlocked the door to the little balcony.

'So you took my advice about the dress.'

She jumped, hair tossing round her shoulders as she whirled to look at him. 'I haven't much else to wear.'

Though his stiff hair glistened with water, he was fully clad, as she'd known and feared he would be. Waistcoat and dark trousers sat close to his narrow waist, and the white shirt was buttoned right up to the strong, smooth neck, one button higher than usual as if to keep her out.

She glanced down at her own skin-tight purple, and shrugged. The shrug made her breasts point themselves blatantly through the purple rib, but all she could do about that was look away and try to ignore them.

'I've got to put something on,' she added, as much to herself as to him.

'And that is exactly the something,' he flung sideways at her as he loped to the door.

'You can't go like this!' she called after him in dismay. '*P-please*, Nikolai!'

'There is something else you need, perhaps?' He paused with his hand on the latch. 'Your journey home? I will fix it for you before I leave.'

'Before you leave where?' she demanded, muddled by distress. 'I mean, where are you going?'

'That,' he retorted simply and cruelly, 'is my business.'

Already he was raising the latch. In another minute he would be out of here and away who knew where. He looked as if he meant never to see her, or even think of her, ever again.

She couldn't bear it; she had to stop him. She dropped

the hanger and rushed over to fling herself between him and the door.

'You can't leave everything like this, Nikolai!'

'No? But we have done what we needed to do.' The dark eyes raked her. 'I have — what did your buffoon friend call it —— ?'

'He isn't my friend; he never was! Don't, please don't repeat his hateful words!'

'I have taken my pleasure,' Nikolai finished, steel-cold. 'I have no further use for you.'

Mallory recoiled, deeply shocked. 'P-please don't say those things,' she begged, hardly knowing what she was saying herself. 'It was bad enough hearing them from Richard. . .'

'The truth hurts, does it?'

'It's not the truth.' And suddenly, pushed to the limit with nothing to lose, she could speak clear and plain. 'It only hurt from him because I once respected him and thought I loved him.'

'So much is your love worth,' he burst out, wolfish with rage in the hard overhead glare, 'that you give it to this. . .this ass's head!'

'But it hurts much worse from you.' Mallory clung doggedly to her own line of argument. 'From you it's like —— ' seeking a way of explaining, she glanced at her drooping rose in its glass ' —— like all the roses withering.'

'The roses withered long ago, dev. . .Mallory Hawthorne. But no, it is worse than that.'

He left the door and loped to the table to pluck the rose from its glass. While she stared stupidly he brandished it at her, drops of water sparkling round it and petals flaking off.

'At least this was real. You never were.'

Mallory shook herself and hurried over to him,

instinctively cupping her hands to catch the petals as they fell. 'Don't torment it, Nikolai. . .'

'Why not? You tormented me from the moment we met.' He hurled the rose in a final drift of petals to the carpet. 'That was the real you which I would not see, though it was there from the start.'

Mallory stared at him, speechless. It was so true. In her early, heady hours of freedom from the burden of being Mallory Hawthorne, she'd tempted and flirted, teased and provoked, and left all the restraint to him. Only as she'd grown to know him, only as her dazzled love for him had broadened into friendship and respect had she ceased to torment him exactly as he described.

'Shameless nakedness and shameless glances, shameless paint and shameless clothing,' the deep voice tore on. 'No wonder you do not like who you are, Mallory Hawthorne.'

She huddled into herself, purple-painted hands up before her pointing breasts. 'This dress is the only one I have.'

'It is what you chose.'

'Without trying it on. . .'

'You knew what you were doing. As you knew what to do over there ——' he pointed to the bed '—though you have pretended all this time to be a virgin——'

'I w-wasn't pretending,' she choked, frantic to clear herself at least on this. 'That was my first time ever.'

'Yes?' The wolfish, taunting eyes blazed down at her. 'And you also truly lost your memory?'

'Oh, God!' She turned away, unable to face the burning hatred in eyes where until now she had seen only gentleness and care. 'I've already explained——'

'You cannot explain away the lies,' he cut in implacably. 'Not one, but many lies. After such lies——' he threw the ugly word at her yet again, a weapon to wound '—why should I believe anything you try to tell me?'

Why indeed? Mallory drooped before him, silent and defenceless as the poor naked rose on the carpet.

'I should never have trusted you at all, after Megan,' he added as if to himself. 'It is not by chance that you look like her——'

'But I'm not like her, I'm *not*,' she interrupted desperately. 'Please don't think that, Nikolai! I'm nobody but me. . .'

'Yes, Megan is past and gone.' Almost, the hard glance softened. 'To think that for a time I was grateful to you for that. To think that for a time I. . .'

He trailed off, his hands stealing out as if against his will to set themselves either side of her waist. Then she was close to him, fitted to the marvellous male length of him, surrounded and overcome by him, taking his lips and giving her own in a kiss which went on and on. . .

A kiss of farewell. She knew that as soon as he freed his mouth from hers, though he held her and gazed hungrily down at her. His palms slid to her arms and down them, caressing her flesh as if they couldn't bear to leave it. They reached her wrists, her hands, her fingers, clung for a moment, then slid over her painted nails and were gone to their own marvellous, different life in which they would never again touch her.

'Perhaps, some day. . .'

He didn't finish, but turned slowly away from her. Grinding the rose-petals underfoot, he moved once more to the door.

'Perhaps what?' she called after him, hating him and loving him and hurting so much she couldn't bear it. 'Some day what?'

'Nothing.' He reached the door, and opened it. 'Only that perhaps, some day——' he lingered with his hand on the latch ' — I will learn not to be taken in by women like you.' Yet still his gaze burned over her features. 'By stag eyes, and ivory skin, and a mouth like an opening rose. . .'

'Did you say all those things to Megan first, then?' she threw at him from the depths of her pain. 'Were they all hers before they were mine?'

His chin thrust out for his vigorous Bulgarian no. 'They were never Megan's, only yours,' he told her quietly. 'Those eyes, that skin, that mouth, they are the tools of your trade, Mallory Hawthorne.'

'What trade?' she asked, outraged.

'The sea-girl trade of deceiving men, I suppose.'

And then he had gone, and the door had closed. When she rushed to wrench it open he was already far down the corridor.

'I don't deceive men, and I don't trade my looks,' she called after him. 'I work in a *bank*, Nikolai Antonov!'

But he didn't turn back, or give any sign of having heard. Presently he rounded a corner and was gone.

He's left me. I'm alone again.

The two facts echoed over and over in the frozen wasteland of her mind as she closed the door. They drifted past her like snow as she swept the naked rose and its poor, trodden petals into her hand and put them on the table. They roared in her ears like an icy wind as she went out to the balcony with her everyday clothes, and hung them to air overnight. They bounced about her like hail as she showered, and removed the purple nail-varnish, and scrubbed off the last of the purple lipstick, and washed out her briefs and hung them to dry. They loomed over her like an iceberg as she remade her lonely bed.

When she put on the rose-russet shirt, now her nightdress, the ice threatened to melt. The scent of

roses and cinnamon prickled round her, and she only
kept back the tears by reminding herself that he hated
this scent as much as he now hated her.

'He's left me,' she said aloud to herself as she
switched off the hateful overhead light.

'I'm alone again,' she added as she settled into bed.

But it was no good; she couldn't conquer her misery
here, of all places. In this bed he was still with her, the
roses and cinnamon now edged by the male musk which
was his real scent, swirling about her to remind her of
that brief unity which was the only one she would ever
have, the only one she ever wanted. . .

So the tears came, and she made no more efforts to
stop them. She could as easily have stopped a tidal
wave. They rolled over her and pulled her this way and
that, one moment stretched on the mattress with her
face buried in the fragrant pillow, the next sitting up to
gasp and keen and rock with her eyes wide to the
miserable dark.

And yet presently they passed, and she was calm
again. She could even switch on the bedside light and go
to the bathroom and bathe her hot eyes. When she had
dried them she waited with the towel in her hand, but it
was all right, they stayed dry. For now, she had no more
tears left to shed.

I'll have to find out where Richard's staying, she
astonished herself by thinking, and get back my passport
and clothes.

She didn't like the idea of seeing Richard without the
bulk of Nikolai protecting her, but it didn't matter.
She'd do it. What was left of her could do anything now,
she decided as she returned to the bed and prepared to
switch out the light.

*Anything but kill myself*. The thought jerked her
upright

How strange, she reflected; it simply never occurred to me.

Everything she had done since he'd left, everything she had planned, all had been for going on *living*, even without him. She'd showered away the heat and dust of her hectic day. She'd hung up her clothes to look as neat as possible when she next wore them. She'd resolved to get back her passport. In every way she had acted like a rational, complete human being with a life to live.

And my credit cards'll be with my passport, she found herself thinking even now. I'll be able to buy a ticket back to the coast, and catch my flight home. . .

But nowhere she'd lived before she'd met Nikolai could possibly be home to her now.

Still, I could buy a flat or something, she decided, pushing away the bleak thought that, without Nikolai, one place was like another. Maybe I could even buy a house in Bulgaria; who knows? I can certainly travel here again, and visit Dragalevtsy. . .

Chasing Nikolai? But she only wanted to see a place dear to this man who had shown her how good life could be. It would never be so good without him, but still it was life, and precious — he'd shown her that, too. She would never wantonly try to throw it away.

'Thank you for that, Nikolai,' she murmured aloud, and switched off her bedside light.

The dark was friendly now, and the scent of musk and cinnamon and roses something to be treasured.

And she hadn't been here a moment, not a second, yet sunlight was brilliant on the patterned curtains.

And who could be calling her on the hotel phone?

Not. . . Could it be. . . ?

Clumsy with haste and sleep, she grabbed the shrilling handset. 'Yes?'

After all it was only the desk-clerk, but with joyful news. 'A gentleman wishes to see you, Miss Howell.'

'Mr Antonov?' She was wide awake, and all the birds in the world were singing. 'Send him up. . .'

'Not Mr Antonov. This gentleman is English, Miss Howell.'

'Oh.' Not all the birds in the world after all, only the sparrows and pigeons and blackbirds of Kazanlük. 'Mr Sherwood? Tell him I'll be right down. . .'

'Not Mr Sherwood,' the clerk patiently corrected her again. 'This is a Mr Hawthorne. . .please?' The last word was in response to some other voice in the background. 'Not Mr, he say, but Detective Inspector Hawthorne to see you, Miss Howell.'

# CHAPTER NINE

'YOU'RE doing *what*?' Detective Inspector Hawthorne leant over their table in the hotel dining-room, his light grey eyes wide with outrage. 'My daughter——' his sharp London voice stressed the word with affronted precision '——travelling on a false passport?'

Mallory had never seen him so angry. Come to think of it, in the year she had shared his flat she'd never seen him angry at all. Always hurrying to whatever he had to do next, he would mostly just grunt in passing, his mind elsewhere.

Now it was she who didn't want to be bothered, and certainly not with this detail he considered important. Sighing, she reminded herself that he and his details were part of the dreary world she had to live in from now on, and dragged her gaze from the entrance by which she had insisted they sit.

'It's not forged or anything. It just isn't mine.'

'So that's all right, then!' His broad forehead creased in a frown as he studied her. 'What's got into you, girl?'

'Nothing. . .' Mallory broke off to lean eagerly forwards, but the tall figure striding down the distant stairs was nobody she knew, nobody she cared about.

She slumped back in her chair. Of course she was glad of her father's tough shrewdness, which had already traced Richard to the bed-and-breakfast where the fully booked hotel had sent him. She was grateful to him for getting back her luggage and passport, but must he ask so many questions? He'd been throwing them at her ever since they'd met at the desk twenty minutes ago.

'How did you know Megan Howell was me, anyway?' she asked, hoping to head him off at last.

Some hope. 'Same initials, the only English person here—you surely didn't think I'd find it hard?' D. I. Hawthorne surveyed her in disgust. 'You make a lousy law-breaker, Mal.'

'I wasn't *trying* to break the law; stop fussing——'

'Stop *what*?' His roar turned every head in the room, and he brought it down to a fast-boiling hiss. 'My own daughter——'

'It's not as if I've left the country on the wretched thing.'

'Only because I've got yours back for you.'

'If you hadn't, I'd have gone and got it myself,' she pointed out, eyes on the people coming and going beyond the restaurant's double doors. 'First thing after breakfast.'

'Oh, yes? And how would you have found where he's staying?' But the hiss cooled a little. 'I know you haven't considered this much lately, my girl, but your father's a trained policeman.'

'It doesn't take a policeman's skills to talk to the desk-clerk,' she countered wearily. 'And stop calling me "your girl".'

'Right, Miss Mallory Hawthorne. . .'

'Now you're being pompous.'

'*Pompous*!' This time he fairly swelled up with rage. 'Why, if you were my son instead of my daughter, I'd——'

'The son you wanted?' Hardened by misery, she could voice this long-held suspicion with perfect calm. 'You had to take what you could get, but you'd rather have had a boy, wouldn't you?'

'No, I wouldn't,' he retorted promptly. 'Your mother——'

'Oh, well, *she'd* accept nothing but a girl on principle.'

'We both wanted *you*, Mal.'

'She'd never settle for. . . What?'

Caught at last by the rare undercurrent of feeling in the hard voice, Mallory forgot her useless watch on the door. As she stared across the table, she was scarcely aware of the waiter putting their breakfasts in front of them.

'From the minute we first saw you, we—er. . .' Her father broke off, looked down, looked back at her. 'We *loved* you, Mal.'

'You've never said a word,' she gasped. 'Not once. . .'

'I take care of you, don't I? I've given you a home this past year, though it hasn't been easy.' He filled his cup, tasted, and pulled a face. 'What kind of cat-pee is this?'

'It's a good cup of tea,' she snapped, defender of everything Bulgarian. 'Just don't put milk in it. Why hasn't it been easy?'

'I'm not used to having a woman about any more, am I? Tea without milk, what next?' he added in a grumbling aside, and drained his cup. 'Your smalls are always drying when I want a shower, you tidy my things out of existence, and—er——' a delicate pause '—if I meet somebody I like, we have to go to her place.'

'I'm twenty-five years old,' Mallory reminded him in renewed astonishment. 'I know the facts of life.'

'And I have my standards where my daughter's concerned.' He poured his next tea, liberally milked as before. 'Which is why I'm here to get you, as you didn't come home when you were told.'

Mallory was silenced. She saw how, in her father's macho terms, it made sense to spend a few days' leave bringing back an erring daughter. And now he was here, she found comfort in the sight of him across the table. That light jacket, his concession to the heat, fitted as well as his usual suits, and his silk tie was elegant as ever. So neat was he, so alert that nobody would have suspected that he'd travelled all night to catch up with her.

'But how did you know I'd be in Kazanlük?' she asked. 'You didn't even go to Duni, just came straight here.'

'Yes, well——' terse as ever, he was guardedly proud of his skill '—if you'd stayed on the line last week, I'd have told you your boyfriend's plans.'

'Don't call him my boyfriend. . . What plans?'

'You know he's banging on doors to make it as a singer?'

'A folk-singer. Yes, I do know about that.'

'Just. You're not fit to be let out, Mal.' Her father shook his aggressively handsome head, and went on. 'He's here to pay out his wife's money to some group of Bulgarian caterwaulers——'

'Bulgarian folk-music's marvellous!' she cut in, bristling.

'Beg its pardon, I'm sure. Anyway, he wants them for back-up on this record he plans to make.' D. I. Hawthorne drank his next tea, pulled another face, and started on his sausages and eggs. 'At least these are eatable.'

'I should think they are,' Mallory retorted. 'So Richard came to Kazanlük to find this group who sang here last night?'

'Who're here for the festival,' her father confirmed with his mouth full. 'And where he was, I expected to find you.' He set his knife and fork together on the empty plate, fierce eyes full on her. 'Which I do, with no gear and a false passport. What the hell've you been up to?'

Mallory looked down at her own barely touched bread and honey. 'Nothing much.'

'Don't give me that. You've found another feller, haven't you? A criminal this time —'

'He *isn't*!' Mallory jerked her head up. 'He's a good man, a *good* man. . .' She found tears splashing down her cheeks, and mopped them angrily with her paper napkin.

Her father made no attempt to comfort her, not even the offer of a hand across the table. The merest flicker of compassion lit the hard features, and was gone.

'C'mon, Mal, get a grip. You were doing so well just now.'

'When?' She was relieved to find that his harshness had stemmed her tears. 'What d'you mean, I was doing well?'

'Back-answering. Showing you could handle yourself.' The light grey eyes surveyed her with reluctant pride. 'I didn't know you had it in you.'

She gaped in amazement. 'You *like* what I've done?'

'Certainly not. But I do like,' he added, cautious as ever in expressing his feelings, 'what it's done to *you*.'

'I suppose,' she began, dazed with this new view of herself, 'I have Nikolai to thank for that.'

'So where is this Nikolai? How come he's left you crying by yourself? C'mon, Mal. Tell.'

'You're just like him, ordering me about. . .'

But when she had finished grumbling, she told. Not of her pretended amnesia — she wouldn't speak of that — but she did explain how she'd left the hotel phone, and at once met another man.

'And then we toured the country. It's been marvellous.'

'False passport and all? If he was so bloody marvellous,' Simon Hawthorne fulminated, 'why the hell didn't he help you get your own stuff from that other toe-rag——?'

'Do you want to hear the rest, or not?'

He simmered down, visibly controlling himself. 'Carry on.'

And she did. Luckily she didn't need to go beyond last night's disastrous encounter. When she falteringly spoke of what Richard had said, D. I. Hawthorne could be silent no longer.

'And this new twerp of yours believed that? What a——'

'If you call him names, I'll leave now,' Mallory cut in, stony and resolved.

She meant it, though it would have felt like losing her father just at the moment when she had found him. Their glances locked across the table, and presently she realised with amazement that she had won. Whatever he thought of Nikolai, from now on he would keep his opinion to himself.

Her victory gave her courage to go on. 'The fact is, I'd already lied to him about. . .about other things, and he knew it.'

'Do you. . .?' Her father's voice was low, careful. 'Do you feel like telling me what they were, these lies you told?'

'Some time, maybe,' she answered in the same low, careful tones. 'When I. . .' She swallowed. 'When I feel better about it. If that ever happens——'

'So!' a new, loved voice thundered. 'You replace me already?'

Mallory jumped, and gazed joyfully upwards. 'Nikolai!'

'You remember me?' Above the usual dark waistcoat

and fresh white shirt his burning eyes, deep-shadowed as if from lack of sleep, swept over her. 'You do not lose your memory with each new lover?'

'Please, please don't talk like that!' She felt her own eyes fill once more. 'I've been watching and watching for you.'

'Watching, ha!' The stiff hair tossed in furious denial. 'When I come here, all I see is your beauty, lighting up the room. . .' He stopped for an angry, baffled moment, then tore on. 'But you! You can see nothing, hear nothing, think of nothing but your new lover——'

'Hold it right there, son.' D. I. Hawthorne's weighty official manner would have stopped an express train. 'I'm not her lover; I'm her old dad.'

Mallory felt her mouth drop open again. 'You never let me call you that, even when I was tiny.'

'Your mum wouldn't, you mean. She always was a snob.'

'You are her father?' Nikolai stared suspiciously from one to the other. 'I see no likeness.'

'Sit down and cool off, and maybe you will.' D. I. Hawthorne leant across the table and pulled out a chair. 'Though I doubt it. My daughter's a right little cracker——'

'Father!' He'd never spoken of her looks before, either.

'—and I'm a hard-bitten old copper,' he went on. 'Mind, I'm flattered you think she might fancy me if we weren't related.'

'Father and daughter.' Nikolai assessed first one, then the other. 'You have come to fetch her? To make her behave?'

'Sit down,' D. I. Hawthorne answered impassively. 'And maybe I'll tell you.'

Nikolai haughtily ignored the order. 'I leave very

soon. I am here only because I remembered I must help this daughter of yours —' he gestured scornfully at Mallory '—whose passport is still with her last lover —'

'He wasn't my lover; he *wasn't*—'

'Forget the passport; I've got it.' Light eyes met dark, and held. 'You think my daughter would go for that scum?'

Mallory was reminded of an old lion warning a young one away from its females. The young one wasn't about to be seen off, but couldn't ignore the challenge. Light and dark eyes held in a contest that went on and on. Then in his usual decisive manner Nikolai lifted the chair, turned it well away from Mallory, and seated himself almost with his back to her.

'I think you do not know what she does?' But he made it a question, not a statement. 'It is often so in your country.'

'I know exactly what she does, or I knew until a week ago. About what's happened since she came here —' the light grey eyes flicked a warning '—I've some questions to ask you.'

'I've told my father how we met,' Mallory put in hastily, 'at Duni, *in the hotel lobby.*'

Would Nikolai go along with her story? She didn't know. The splendid head briefly turned her way, but the fire-dark gaze, in the moment it rested on hers, was unreadable as ever.

'If I had known that she has such a father,' he commented to Simon Hawthorne, 'I would have worried less about her.'

'I'm a grown-up person,' Mallory protested, 'and I'm sitting right by you —'

'That's some worrying, mate.' Her father hadn't even

glanced her way. 'Encouraging her to travel on false documents.'

Nikolai was silent for a moment. The dark eyes had hooded, the long mouth pulled in, giving the handsome features all the closed-up strength of a hard bargainer.

'That was wrong,' he pronounced at last, clearly having decided that he would concede the point. 'I am sorry for it.'

'You are?' Simon Hawthorne wavered a little, as if he hadn't expected the apology. 'Well, I suppose that's something.'

'I can only say——' Nikolai shot Mallory a brief, furious glare ' — that I was in love with her.'

'You were what?' She felt as if all the breath had been knocked out of her. 'You never said——'

'So that's what you call love, is it?' her father's cynical tones cut through hers. 'Well, if you're another one leading my daughter up the garden path, I'll——'

'What is this leading up the garden path?' Nikolai's deep voice rode down the warning. 'It means to deceive, does it not?'

'With Sherwood, it meant not letting on he was married.'

'She did not know this about her Robin Hood?'

'Her who? Oh.' The light grey gaze hardened in contempt. 'Not till Duni she didn't. I told her when she first arrived.'

'That's why I. . .' Mallory hesitated, on dangerous ground but unable to keep quiet. 'Why I walked away. . .'

'She'd that much sense,' Simon Hawthorne rasped at Nikolai. 'Whether's she's done any better with you, we'll have to see.'

'Father!' Mallory exclaimed. 'I haven't. . . He isn't. . .'

'I doubt it, because she hasn't the savvy of a new-laid egg. And no wonder, seeing she never goes out,' D. I. Hawthorne informed his fellow-male. 'Twenty-five years old, prettiest little thing in London, and what does she do every night?'

'She went out with her Robin Hood, I suppose?'

'Nah, she only met him about a month ago. Before that she sat home every night and studied.'

'You want me to get on at the bank, don't you, Father?'

'Blasted exams, that's all she ever thought about.'

'Exams.' Unsure of himself at last, Nikolai turned wondering eyes on Mallory. 'That is not what I heard.'

'So I gather. And have you thought who you heard it from?' D. I. Hawthorne was now in his element. 'I wouldn't take a handshake from that Sherwood, let alone his word about a woman.'

After a long silence, Nikolai pushed his chair back from the table and at last turned fully to Mallory. 'You loved him?'

She put her hands to her burning cheeks, but met the fire-dark eyes full on. 'I. . . I thought I did.'

'And now?'

'How could I possibly? Even if he'd stayed nice. . .'

'You see? Raw as a new-laid egg.' Simon Hawthorne's gritty tones reminded them that they were not alone. 'That slimy bastard was never "nice", Mal,' he went on pityingly. 'Why d'you think I asked questions about him in the first place?'

'But he *was*, Father.' She stood her ground before these two formidable men. 'He didn't grope, or even make remarks. . .'

She trailed off, defeated. How could the kind, quiet person who'd brought her to Duni have become last night's lying monster?

'He called you a groupie,' Nikolai reminded her. 'He listed the men you had lain with. . .'

'My little Mal?' Simon Hawthorne was suddenly all father. 'I'll murder him. . .'

'Not if I am there first.' Nikolai had already sprung with bleak purpose from his chair.

'Wh-where are you going?' Mallory asked him in alarm.

'To find this Robin Hood,' he informed her over his shoulder, 'and break his guitar in his teeth.'

'And then stuff it up his. . .nose. Wait for me, son!' Simon Hawthorne was also on his feet. 'I know how to get there; we can go in my car.'

'Sit down, both of you!' Mallory exhorted in alarm. 'Please!'

But, except as a cause for war, she was once more invisible.

'You're Nikolai, aren't you?' Her father caught up, and offered a well-kept hand. 'You can call me Si — all my mates do.'

'Mates means friends, does it not?' Nikolai thought for a moment, then took the offered hand. 'How do you do, Si? My friends call me Malko.'

'Mal and Malko.' The light grey eyes swept mockingly over Nikolai's height, and back to where Mallory sat rigid. 'Seems like it was meant, doesn't it?'

'*Nothing's* meant,' she began, hot with embarrassment now as well as everything else. 'Nothing's been said. . . Come back!'

But already they were off. For a moment she stared after the two retreating backs, the taller with the loose stride of the athlete, the chunkier with the no-nonsense walk of one whose job often took him among people who were dangerous.

'If you can't beat them, join them,' she murmured to herself.

She stood up with such speed that she almost toppled her chair. If she didn't hurry, they'd be into her father's hired car and away without her.

She caught up with them at the hotel entrance. Nikolai, holding the swing-door for her father, stiffened when he saw her.

'This is man's business, *devoika*.'

'I don't know how you can say that,' she retorted, 'seeing you're doing this because of me. . .*hell*!'

Through the still-open door, across the pavement, she saw Richard paying off a taxi. Wearing tweeds, he was less absurd, but still bleary, which wasn't surprising, she thought in that frozen moment. Apart from last night's fracas, which had left that bruise on his chin, it must have been a shock to wake before dawn to D. I. Hawthorne in interrogating mode. And now he had worse to face. . .

'Excuse me, *devoika*.'

Nikolai, too, had seen the new arrival. The next thing Mallory knew, he had pushed through the swing-door in front of her and left it to close in her face.

By the time she had it open again, and herself out in the rose-scented air, things were already happening. The taxi had gone, and on the edge of the pavement Nikolai and her father both seemed to have expanded and darkened, two figures of revenge with Richard caught between. Early morning passers-by stared with frank Slav interest, but none stayed to watch, thank heaven.

'Do you mind?' Richard was blustering when Mallory reached them. 'I've nothing more to say to either of you.'

'You think not?' Nikolai demanded, quietly murderous.

'Please, Nikolai——'

'Shut up, Mal. But she's right, son; that's not the way. I'm wondering,' D. I. Hawthorne continued, narrow-eyed, 'if we can get him for slander.'

'Do that—it'd be great publicity,' Richard taunted hoarsely. 'It's good headline stuff, what I could tell a court about this little alley-cat. . .'

Flinching as from a blow, Mallory saw Nikolai's fist draw back. She prepared to spring in front of him, but already her father had caught the strong wrist and held it fast.

'Fair makes your foot itch, doesn't it?' he commented with a grin, and to Richard, 'All right, we'll settle for an apology.'

'No way!'

'Let me go,' Nikolai ordered. 'I will only hit him once. . .'

'No!'

That was Mallory, but nobody was listening. Her father had spoken at the same time.

'Give us a chance, mate.'

'Father, you are *not* to call him that. . .'

'Kindly stop this nonsense.' Richard shot a hunted glance at his watch. 'I'm meeting somebody. . .'

'So let's be having that apology,' D. I. Hawthorne calmly instructed, still hindering Nikolai. 'Or you'll be late.'

'Get lost!'

'I intend to, but not before I've rung your wife.'

'Father!' Mallory cried, stricken. 'You can't do that!'

Nikolai slowly dropped his fist. 'That would be to hurt an innocent woman. . .'

'It's time she knew,' Simon Hawthorne retorted, and

once more addressed Richard. 'I've got it all here.' He tapped his pocket. 'The Seabrook Hotel last year, Torquay last summer, Duni last week with my little Mal——'

'I'll never speak to you again, Father——'

'Quiet, Mal.' At last D. I. Hawthorne deigned to heed his daughter. 'It won't come to that.'

'Won't it?' Richard's bruise was suddenly livid, his eyes like trapped insects in the dirty pink of his face. 'You can't prove a thing.'

'Proving things is my job, sunshine. I wonder how your wife'll feel about funding this record you want to make,' the calm tones ground on, 'when she hears how you play away from home?'

'She. . .she won't believe you.'

'Won't she? I take that as a challenge——'

'All right!' Richard burst out in a fury. 'I. . .' He gagged, then got it out. 'I *apologise*. . .'

'For the lies I told,' D. I. Hawthorne prompted.

'They weren't. . . All right.' The insect eyes shifted from his tormentor's rock-hard chill to Nikolai's towering heat, and down to Mallory's shrinking revulsion. 'I've hardly kissed her—not what I call kissing. Nor has anyone else—it's a standing joke. . .'

'So!' Nikolai grabbed him by the shirt. 'We will see who laughs now. . .'

'Please, please stop!' Mallory tried to fling herself between the two, but once more it was her father who parted them.

'Haven't you heard about "Don't get mad, get even", son?'

Slowly, reluctantly, nostrils still distended and eyes blazing, Nikolai released his grip. With a great show of dusting himself down, Richard tried to step to one side, but the impassive D. I. Hawthorne was there before him.

'What's this about a standing joke?'

'How nobody could get into her——' Richard censored out some coarseness '——could get near her. That's why I bet——'

'You *bet* about me?' Mallory interrupted, stricken.

'With your looks, you have to expect to be talked about,' Richard threw at her as if it were her fault. 'I said I could get you to bed, going softly-softly. They gave me six weeks.'

'Ugh!'

Mallory huddled herself together against the world which had such people in it. Then a strong arm drew her to a broad chest, a powerful barrier between her and the casual indecency they had just heard, and Nikolai waved her father to silence.

'Why did you speak such lies? She has done you no harm. . .'

'No harm!' Richard echoed, full of incredulous self-pity. 'I haven't slept since she left, worrying what had become of her!' The insect eyes sought Mallory's. 'You've started me drinking again, you know that? Just when I'd got it beaten——'

'A man drinks by his own choice,' Nikolai cut in, stone-faced. 'Or he is not a man.'

'Leave it, Nikolai.' Mallory's father took over. 'It's never their fault; that's the first rule with trash like this.'

'And then there you were as if nothing had happened,' Richard tore on, getting it all out now he'd started, 'with lover-boy. . .'

'Didn't you say you were meeting somebody?' D. I. Hawthorne asked with chill disgust. 'Don't keep them waiting on our account—and I hope,' he added as

Richard scuttled over the pavement into the hotel, 'they've got the disinfectant ready.'

Mallory blinked, hardly able to believe that it was over, her name cleared. And the day wasn't even far on, the sun barely over the buildings on the other side of the street.

'I'd better go up and pack,' she said reluctantly. 'I've a plane to catch, if I can get to Burgas airport in time. . .'

'You haven't,' her father contradicted flatly. 'Your manky friend cancelled the booking. He's going from Sofia later.'

'Well, I must get back somehow,' she pointed out. 'I only had a week's leave.'

'We will talk about that,' Nikolai told her.

'You'll talk to me first,' Simon Hawthorne said unexpectedly. 'For a start, can you keep her?'

'There you go again!' Mallory cried, crimson-faced. 'When we haven't so much as —— '

'Come with us to Sofia, and I will show you how my income is made up.' As before, Nikolai was completely at home with this male bargaining. 'You may also see my flat, which is more than big enough for two, and the house I am building. . .'

'Right, I'll take you up on that. But not yet.' Simon Hawthorne glanced at his watch. 'I've a week's leave, and, seeing Mal's sorted out, I might as well find a beach to lie on.' The light grey eyes sought Nikolai's. 'I hear the Black Sea coast's quite decent?'

'Decent!' Nikolai echoed indignantly. 'Why, it is. . .it is. . .'

'It's a part of heaven,' Mallory finished for him. 'The whole country is — you'll see.'

'Yes, well, I'll let you know. Let's have your Sofia address, son, and we'll fix a meeting later.'

'You leave your daughter so soon?' Nikolai asked, puzzled. 'I do not understand the father who could do this.'

'She'll be all right.' The light grey eyes, used to judging character at a glance, flicked over him. 'She's in good hands.'

'You won't even spend an evening with us?' Mallory murmured, without hope. 'Just to get acquainted?'

'It isn't me you need to get acquainted with, is it?'

'No, I already know you,' she answered with a sigh. 'And you'll never change, will you?'

After that it seemed no time before they waved her father off. Her luggage transferred from his car, her newly restored passport safe in her newly restored handbag, she turned to Nikolai as the hired car disappeared in the distance.

'He's what you'd call a man of action.'

'He is your father.' Clearly, to Nikolai the relationship was sacred. 'And in his way, he loves you.'

'Yes,' she agreed, cheering up. 'But I'm sorry about those things he said, Nikolai. You know——' she couldn't meet his eyes '—about your income and all that. . .'

'But that was exactly as it should be,' Nikolai responded in puzzled tones. 'When *I* have daughters, I will do exactly thus.'

'Perhaps it's lucky that your lot only has boys, then. . .'

She got no further. He had lightly touched her waist to guide her along with him. The tiny contact affected both with equal force, and they stopped together in mid-pavement. Fighting for composure in the everyday morning world, Mallory licked her lips, but that, too, was a mistake. She saw the fire-dark eyes kindle and narrow as he struggled for control.

'Let us go, *devoika*.'

And they did. He had long since cleared his room and paid the bill. To collect her few things from her room and put them in the car was the work of a moment.

'Not an open rose in sight,' Mallory observed as they sped through the rose-fields in the strengthening sunlight.

'They have been picked, but their perfume lives.' He kept his eyes on the road. 'Soon we come to the Georgi Dimitrov Dam.'

'And then?'

He shrugged. 'Kalofer, Karlovo, Kurnare, Rosini, the rose-towns. Then other towns. Then Sofia. . .' He slowed the car.

'I have to get back to my job, Nikolai.'

'You will telephone, and ask for another week.'

'Only a week?' She tried to hide her disappointment, sitting forwards as he nosed the car off the road and down a tiny rutted track between the rose-bushes. 'Where are we going now?'

'I cannot speak of these things while I drive.' He switched the engine off, the scented foliage closing them in. 'First —' he held stiffly apart from her, hands white-knuckled on his lap ' — I am sorry I believed those lies of you.'

'I lied, too,' she almost whispered. 'I'm sorry for that. I wanted so much to stay with you. . .'

'I also. We were both to blame.' But still he held off, not giving so much as a glance in her direction. 'From now on, we will be honest togther.'

'Yes. So I have to tell you. . .' She swallowed, stared past the green spires of the rose-bushes to the distant blue of the Balkan Range, and tried again. 'You like my father, don't you?'

'In his way——' Nikolai chose his words carefully '—he is a good man.'

'Yes. Well. . .' She breathed deep, and brought it out in a rush. 'He's not my father. And my mother's not my mother.'

'What is this?' He turned his head at last in a questioning frown. 'You were not born in the usual way?'

'Not in the usual way, no. . .'

He sat impassive while she told what she must tell. She stole the occasional glance at him, but the fine profile, bronze-gold in the dappled shadows, stayed unmoving. His only reaction came when she made guesses, as she so often did, about the man who had begotten her.

'Maybe he was Bulgarian.'

'I think not.'

'Don't you want me as your compatriot, Nikolai?'

'I do not want a compatriot who would father a child with so little thought.'

'He'd never know. It must happen all the time.'

'And then to leave her, his daughter. . .'

'Father and Ma were good to me, for all they divorced.'

'Divorce also?' Still he did not turn to her, but now at last he reached out, and with infinite tenderness smoothed her cheek with the back of one finger. 'Unlucky indeed, *lyubima*.'

'You called me that once before,' she murmured, breathlessly resisting the waves of sweetness which spread through her from that tiny caress. 'What does it mean?'

'Come to Dragalevtsy, *lyubima*.' Still he would not tell her what the word meant, though he used it again as he pushed all of his fingers through her hair and held the back of her head in his cupped hand. 'I have family enough there for two.'

'I suppose — ' nestling against his hand, she forced herself to be practical ' — I *could* phone the bank.'

'I will help.' His hand left her as if he, too, was trying to think only of everyday affairs. 'And then you will write your resignation.'

'I'll do what?' Startled, she turned to stare at him.

'You cannot be in two places at once,' he pointed out with his usual common-sense air.

'But I can't give up my job just like that. . .'

'I have a job for you.'

'Yes?' She waited, breathless.

'You will keep my accounts.'

'Oh.' Cast down, she tried to take an interest. 'You've decided what to do with your money, then?'

'Almost.' He dismissed the question. 'Your real job will come. . .' He broke off, magnificent head on one side, straight eyebrows drawn together, smoke-dark eyes distant as he worked out some calculation or other. 'After Easter next year.'

'Why then?' she asked, puzzled.

'Many reasons. *Koledouvane* at Christmas, *Martenitzas* in March, *Lararouvane* in April — '

'Hang on!' she laughingly interrupted the flow of strange words. 'What are all those things?'

'Festivals we must celebrate together. Then at Easter we go to the cathedral. You must see our Orthodox Easter.' He turned to her, smoke-dark eyes alight. 'All rejoice together, and the church shines like a part of heaven.'

'Another part of heaven,' she murmured, enchanted.

'And at midnight, the cathedral doors are opened for the Patriarch to bear out the sacred light.' Still holding carefully away, he kept his eyes intent on hers. 'We all light candles from it and carry them away, candles in every street. . . That——' the deep voice sank to a passionate murmur '—is when we will begin life anew. When we have brought home the light.'

'A candle-flame?' She had to voice her uncertainty. 'Does it blow out?'

'Easily. As easily as a life.'

She couldn't meet those dark, steadfast eyes any longer, but had to gaze ahead to the blue mountains. 'If I said I'll never, ever do such a dangerous thing as walking into the sea without thinking again, will you believe me?'

'While you are with me you will not!' he agreed, arrogant as ever.

'I thought I was alone again last night.' She faced him, glad to tell the whole truth. 'I was completely miserable—and yet I got on with my life. I always will now—thanks to you.'

'Then I think, *devoika*, that we will bring home the light together.'

But still he did not touch her, and she knew why. This was not the time for the hot urgency of the flesh, not yet.

'And where will it be, Nikolai?' She held quite still, letting his eyes take hers. 'Where will home be?'

'Your home will be wherever I am, *devoika*. And mine,' he added, soft as a sigh, 'will be wherever you are.'

And now at last she was in his arms, his hard mouth on hers, his hard body sheltering hers as it always would. The heat of the flesh leapt and almost consumed them, but not quite.

'We must go from here.' He put her away from him. 'The roses are gathered for today, but this is a service road only. . .'

'Not yet,' she begged. 'Please let's get out and be among them for a minute.'

'Very well, *devoika*. But only for a minute.'

Out among the waist-high, shoulder-high bushes, she breathed up the swooning, scented air. 'Where do we go next, Nikolai?'

'To Dragalevtsy,' he said promptly. 'You will stay with my parents until we marry.'

'And will we have to—' she looked about at the carefully riotous bushes '—to hold back from each other all that time?'

'Most certainly. They would tolerate nothing less.'

'Then all I'm to know about. . .about love—' she stole a sidelong glance at the dear, defiant head, then reached up to run a daring finger through the dear, springy hair '—is how you were last night?'

'That was bad, what I did then.' He spoke with difficulty, the smoke-dark eyes aflame. 'I took a virgin, I know that now, took her in anger and gave no pleasure in return.'

'You gave pleasure, Nikolai,' she said simply. 'Even then.'

'But still, that is not how it should be.'

'So how should it be?' She put her arms round his neck, and gazed up into the fire-dark eyes. 'Show me.'

'We are among the roses, *devoika*.' The murmur was torn from him, his hands clenched at his sides. 'The roses are a crop.'

'You'll be careful of them.' She glanced round at the few tight pink buds which remained on the bushes. 'You'll show them how to open, and blossom. . .'

After that there were no more words. The long grass between the bushes received them, the green sprays waved, the ghosts of gathered roses caressed, and, somewhere in the blue above, a lark sang. The thread of

song wound higher and more joyous until Mallory could
no longer tell the bird's ecstasy from her own, and
soared with it and with Nikolai, over the roses, over the
mountains, over the rim of the turning earth.

And soon the singing was done, the bird gone. But
Nikolai stayed with her, tender and scolding in the
scented air.

'Always you tempt me, *devoika*.' He walked her to
the car with his strong, springy hand wrapped round
hers. 'Anyone might have come along and seen us.'

'No, they wouldn't,' she contradicted, invincible with
happiness. 'We were hidden by roses.'

'Roses are not enough. You will have to be more
respectable than this, *lyubima*, when you are
Bulgarian.'

'How can I ever be Bulgarian,' she teased lazily, at
peace with all creation, 'if you won't tell me the
language?'

He took her other hand and held it tight, facing her
among the roses. 'I will tell you the language.'

'Right.' She raised her eyes to his. 'What's *lyubima*?'

'It means "my darling".' He kissed one of her hands,
then the other. 'It means my most beloved in all the
world.'

# Welcome to Europe

**BULGARIA** — 'land of the roses'

Bulgaria is a land of contrasts, with long, sandy beaches and a warm blue sea, mountains and rolling farmland, and attractive towns steeped in history. And the Valley of the Roses, overflowing with fragrance and colour in May and June, and bathing in the sunny, warm climate, has to be one of the most romantic settings in Europe.

## THE ROMANTIC PAST

It is sometimes said that the **Danube basin**, which is between Bulgaria and Romania, was the cradle of the human race. Archaeological finds have shown that there were certainly people living there as far back as 6000 BC. The Bulgarian State itself was founded in 681.

The **Cyrillic alphabet**, which is used by the Bulgarians, Russians and Serbs, was created in Bulgaria in the ninth century AD by two Bulgarian monks, Cyril and Methodius.

Bulgaria was conquered by the Ottomans (the Turks) in 1396, and remained under their dominance until 1877. Two of Bulgaria's most heroic figures are **Vasil Levsky** and **Hristo Botev**, freedom fighters who lost their lives while fighting for Bulgaria's revolution.

There are many monuments to the battles and uprisings in Bulgaria while it was being ruled by the Turks. One of the most famous is at the **Shipka Pass**, where some of the fiercest battles were fought. There is a large monument commemorating the Russian troops and Bulgarian volunteers who fought so bravely against the far superior forces of the Turks.

The capital city of Bulgaria is **Sofia**. One story claims that the city got its name from the Emperor Justinian's daughter Sofia, who was cured of a terrible sickness by the healing mineral waters there. Her father, overcome with gratitude, promptly renamed the city after her.

Tradition is part of the lifestyle of all Bulgarians, and there are many folk festivals and customs. We know February fourteenth as Valentine's Day, but in Bulgaria it is Wine-grower's Day, when wine-growers dress in their best clothes, prune their vines, and sprinkle them with wine for a good harvest.

Traditional marriage customs are still practised in Bulgaria today. After the wedding ceremony, it is traditional for the bridesmaids and the bridegroom's men to dance the **rûchenitsa** away from the church. On the following Monday the groom's relatives visit the bride's mother and do the same dance. At the same time, the bride leaves her new home with her husband for the first time and fetches water, which she offers to her mother, while the villagers dance the **rûchenitsa**.

## THE ROMANTIC PRESENT — pastimes for lovers. . .

There can be few more romantic places to visit in May and June than the Valley of the Roses, or **Rosova Dolina**, where hundreds of thousands of roses are in bloom. If you're there for the Rose Festival, you'll be able to enjoy the colourful procession and carnival. But if you want to see the roses being picked you'll have to be up early — the picking is done between dawn and about eight a.m., as the rose petals lose up to fifty per cent of their oil once the sun gets too high.

Bulgaria's capital, **Sofia**, has enough interesting sights to keep you busy for days. The **National History Museum**, where you can see some of the most exciting early finds in Europe and beautiful enamelled jewellery, is well worth a visit. Or why not take a chairlift up **Mount Vitosha** to enjoy the scenic views?

Away from the bustle of sightseeing in **Sofia**, you and your partner can relax by walking hand in hand in the city's beautiful **Južen Park**. Or, close to **Lenin Square**, where you can see a monument to Lenin, you'll find a charming little church and an open-air café where you can enjoy a refreshing drink — perhaps one of the delicious natural fruit juices which Bulgaria exports all over Europe.

And if you think you can hear the sound of bells ringing, the chiming is probably coming from a monument dedicated to peace and the children of the world, which is situated at the foot of **Mount Vitosha**. There is a collection of bells of every shape and size from eighty-nine countries.

If it's total relaxation you're after, lying on one of Bulgaria's **Black Sea** beaches is hard to beat. And don't miss a swim in the 'hospitable sea' — so called because it's warm, clear and has no tides. Not far away from the resort of **Duni** is the attractive fishing port of **Sozopol**, the oldest Greek settlement on the Black Sea. With its picturesque old buildings and narrow cobbled streets, it's a perfect setting for romance.

For an enjoyable change, why not tickle your sense of humour in **Gabrovo**? This town is twinned with Aberdeen in Scotland, and its inhabitants are famous for their sense of humour. There's even a **House of Humour** with over 100,000 humorous items from around the world!

After a busy day sightseeing, what better way to relax than by enjoying a typical Bulgarian meal? You might like to start your meal in the traditional way, with a glass of plum or grape brandy — *Slivova*. Afterwards you can enjoy dishes such as **Shopska Salad** — a mixture of tomatoes, cucumbers, peppers and parsley with cheese grated on them — or *kavarma* — individual casseroles of pork or veal with onion and mushrooms. For dessert, Bulgarian fresh fruit is simply wonderful, while you won't get better yoghurt anywhere in the world!

Evening entertainment shouldn't be too hard to find, for Bulgaria is known as the land of song. Try to catch some of the folk-singing and dancing, done in national costume, while you're there. And if you're in **Sofia**, the **State Opera House** is renowned for its excellent performances.

You're sure to want a memento of Bulgaria, and what could be more fitting than **rose-oil** or **rose water**? The sweet fragrance is guaranteed to remind you of your holiday every time you use it.

## DID YOU KNOW THAT. . .?

* Bulgaria is the major world supplier of **rose-oil**, used in the manufacturing of perfume.

* the Bulgarians invented yoghurt, which they call *kiselo mleko*.

* the Bulgarians have a unique custom of shaking the head to show agreement and nodding to say no.

* Bulgaria has a population of only **nine million** in a country about four fifths the size of England.

* the way to say 'I love you' in Bulgarian is '*Az te obicham*'.

**LOOK OUT FOR TWO TITLES EVERY
MONTH IN OUR SERIES OF
EUROPEAN ROMANCES:**


**ROMAN SPRING:** Sandra Marton (Italy)
Nicolo Sabitini *claimed* that his interest in Caroline was
merely that of an employer. So why did he seem to be
taking over her life?

**LOVE OR NOTHING:** Natalie Fox (Balearics)
Ruth had loved — and lost — once on the beautiful island
of Majorca. But, this time she was determined to win
Fernando's heart once and for all. . .

**WEST OF BOHEMIA:** Jessica Steele: (Czechoslovakia)
On a mission to help her sister, Fabia travelled to
Czechoslovakia to try and interview the arrogant Ven
Gajdusek. But would he see through her deception?

**SICILIAN SPRING:** Sally Wentworth (Sicily)
Bryony had sworn off men — but could she resist Rafe
Cavalleri's devastating Italian charm?

# MILLS & BOON

## CHRISTMAS KISSES...

Melt your heart with
MILLS & BOON

## ...THE GIFT OF LOVE

Four exciting new Romances to melt your heart this Christmas
from some of our most popular authors.

| | |
|---|---|
| ROMANTIC NOTIONS — | Roz Denny |
| TAHITIAN WEDDING — | Angela Devine |
| UNGOVERNED PASSION — | Sarah Holland |
| IN THE MARKET — | Day Leclaire |

Available November 1993     *Special Price only £6.99*

*Available from W. H. Smith, John Menzies, Martins, Forbuoys,
most supermarkets and other paperback stockists.
Also available from Mills & Boon Reader Service, FREEPOST, PO Box 236,
Thornton Road, Croydon, Surrey CR9 9EL. (UK Postage & Packing free)*

# TWO HEARTS...

## ...WORLDS APART

Childhood sweethearts, they'd shared a wild and reckless lov
when Rachel was just seventeen. Now, years later, Tommy Le
could still excite her like no other man. Perhaps this time the
could make it work, in spite of his reputation and the loc
gossip...or was Rachel just chasing a wistful memory from th
past?

**Read *THE HELLION*—an unforgettable love story from the
*New York Times* bestselling author of *Vows*, *Bygones* and
*Spring Fancy*.**

AVAILABLE NOW                                    PRICED £3.

# WORLDWIDE

*Available from W. H. Smith, John Menzies, Martins, Forbuoys,
most supermarkets and other paperback stockists.
Also available from Worldwide Reader Service, PO Box 236,
Thornton Road, Croydon, Surrey CR9 9EL. (UK Postage & Packing free)*

# ESCAPE INTO ANOTHER WORLD...

## ...With Temptation Dreamscape Romances

Two worlds collide in 3 very special Temptation titles, guaranteed
to sweep you to the very edge of reality.

The timeless mysteries of reincarnation, telepathy and earthbound
spirits clash with the modern lives and passions of ordinary men
and women.

Available November 1993                    Price £5.55

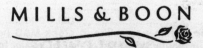

*Available from W. H. Smith, John Menzies, Martins, Forbuoys,*
*most supermarkets and other paperback stockists.*
*Also available from Mills & Boon Reader Service, FREEPOST, PO Box 236,*
*Thornton Road, Croydon, Surrey CR9 9EL. (UK Postage & Packing free)*

# Next Month's Romances

Each month you can choose from a wide variety of romance with Mills & Boon. Below are the new titles to look out for next month, why not ask either Mills & Boon Reader Service or your Newsagent to reserve you a copy of the titles you want to buy – just tick the titles you would like and either post to Reader Service or take it to any Newsagent and ask them to order your books.

| *Please save me the following titles:* | | Please tick | √ |
|---|---|---|---|
| **TO TAME A WILD HEART** | Emma Darcy | | |
| **ISLAND ENCHANTMENT** | Robyn Donald | | |
| **A VALENTINE FOR DAISY** | Betty Neels | | |
| **PRACTISE TO DECEIVE** | Sally Wentworth | | |
| **FLAME ON THE HORIZON** | Daphne Clair | | |
| **ROMAN SPRING** | Sandra Marton | | |
| **LOVE OR NOTHING** | Natalie Fox | | |
| **CLOSE CAPTIVITY** | Elizabeth Power | | |
| **TOTAL POSSESSION** | Kathryn Ross | | |
| **LOST LADY** | Lee Wilkinson | | |
| **GIFT-WRAPPED** | Victoria Gordon | | |
| **NOT SUCH A STRANGER** | Liza Hadley | | |
| **COLOURS OF LOVE** | Rosalie Henaghan | | |
| **CHECKMATE** | Peggy Nicholson | | |
| **TOMORROW'S MAN** | Sue Peters | | |
| **OF RASCALS AND RAINBOWS** | Marcella Thompson | | |

If you would like to order these books in addition to your regular subscription from Mills & Boon Reader Service please send £1.80 per title to: Mills & Boon Reader Service, Freepost, P.O. Box 236, Croydon, Surrey, CR9 9EL, quote your Subscriber No:.................................... (If applicable) and complete the name and address details below. Alternatively, these books are available from many local Newsagents including W.H.Smith, J.Menzies, Martins and other paperback stockists from 5 November 1993.

Name:..............................................................................................

Address:..........................................................................................

...............................................................Post Code:..........................

**To Retailer: If you would like to stock M&B books please contact your regular book/magazine wholesaler for details.**

You may be mailed with offers from other reputable companies as a result of this application. If you would rather not take advantage of these opportunities please tick box ☐